MW01108215

FIRESIDE LOVE

S.L. STERLING

Fireside LOVE

USA TODAY BESTSELLING AUTHOR
S.L. STERLING

Fireside Love

Copyright © 2020 by S.L. Sterling

All rights reserved. Without limiting the rights under copyright reserved about, no part of this publication may be reproduced, stored in, or introduced into a retrieval system, or transmitted in any form or by any means (mechanical, electronic, photocopying, recording, or otherwise) without the prior written permission of both the copyright owner and the above publisher of the book. This is a work of fiction. Any references to historical events, real people, or real places are used fictitiously. Other names, characters, places, and events are products of the author's imagination, and any resemblance to actual events or places or persons, living or dead, is entirely coincidental. Disclaimer: This book contains mature content not suitable for those under the age of 18. It involves strong language and sexual situations. All parties portrayed in sexual situations are consenting adults over the age of 18.

Paperback ISBN: 978-1-989566-11-4

Ebook ISBN: 978-1-989566-12-1

Editor: Brandi Aquino, Editing Done Write

Cover Design: Kim Bailey, Bailey Cover Boutique

1

Kristy

I SAT DOODLING figure eights on the paper that sat in front of me. Tom's voice was sounding more like nails on a chalkboard than ever before. I swore this day was never going to end, and the more he droned on, the more I was convinced I was right. Who the hell calls a meeting at three in the afternoon on a Friday, for goodness' sake. I glanced up at the clock. For a meeting that was only supposed to take a half an hour, my boss sure was winded. He had been going on nonstop for close to an hour and fifteen minutes, and all I could think of was cracking open a bottle of wine and vegging on my couch.

"Everyone, thank you for your time and have a great weekend," Tom, my boss and ex-boyfriend, called out. I glanced up and caught him watching me, giving me a half smile. I dropped my eyes back to the form in front of me.

Jen smacked me in the arm, grabbing my attention. "Let's get out of here," she said, scooping up the papers that sat in front of her.

I glanced around the room. Half of the people were already out the door, and here I was still sitting here doodling, while my ex stood there trying to get my attention. I quickly shoved all the notes into a pile, gave Tom a look, and followed Jen out of the boardroom and back to our offices.

"Honestly, a late-Friday afternoon meeting that really could have been summed up over an email. That was a complete and total waste of time. I could have been halfway home by now," I mumbled as we stepped out of the elevator.

"I know. I swear that man does this on purpose. Seems it's every single Friday night," Jen replied. "Do you have any plans for the weekend?"

"The usual, you know: drown my sorrows in a bottle of wine and shove my face with sweets." We both laughed as we made our way back to our offices.

"That sounds delightful. I'll see you Monday?"

"Yep, I will be here."

I shut the door to my office and jumped behind my computer to send out my final few emails of the day before I packed up my bag. Even though I had zero plans, I was happy it was Friday. I was simply happy to have a couple of days to myself and not have to come into this hellhole I called a job.

My job hadn't always been bad. At one time, I'd actually liked it here. Then I started seeing Tom, my boss, which hadn't been the best idea I'd had. We had dated last summer, probably one of the best summers I'd ever had. Then fall came, he had gotten a new assistant, and things started to get rocky. My performance at work slowed, and suddenly, instead of being praised as one of the best employees, I quickly flew to the bottom of his list. Not only did it cause strain here at the job, but it caused strain on our relationship.

One afternoon, I found out why I had been placed on the bottom of his list, and it wasn't due to my work ethic. I'd gone up to see Tom in his office like usual to finalize our plans for the weekend. His assistant wasn't at her desk when I arrived. I really didn't think anything of it. I just knocked and walked into his office, like I normally did at the end of every Friday. What I saw when I walked into his office I wish I could unsee. His assistant sat on his desk, her skirt pulled up around her thighs, and there in between her legs was Tom.

I could barely believe my eyes, and I instantly felt sick as she hung her head back to moan, I let out a gasp as I covered my mouth. They both looked in my direction, her immediately pulling at her skirt to cover herself up, while he begged me to let him explain. I could feel the heat on my face and took off running toward the elevator.

Tom ran after me, begging for my forgiveness, causing a huge scene. I went home that Friday, had a good cry, and contemplated reporting him to Human Resources. Instead, on Sunday, I called him at home and broke up with him. He's begged me for another chance, but I told him the damage was already done and to keep his distance. Now for the past year and a half I have been subjected to his last-minute meetings, along with looks that no boss should be giving his employee.

I finished packing my bag and was just about to throw it over my shoulder when, out of the corner of my eye, I saw Tom walking slowly down the hall. I rolled my eyes. "Please don't stop. Please don't stop," I mumbled to myself.

The door to my office pushed open and Tom stuck his head in. "Kristy, don't forget to go over the final images for the magazine layout this weekend. I'd like to have them in my hands by Sunday night."

I sucked in a breath and pasted a fake smile across my face. "Sure thing." He had been doing this to me since we had broken up, finding some way to make me work the entire weekend on something. I had been the one who complied, but now I was getting tired of it.

He nodded. "Have a good weekend, Kristy." He waved and went to continue his way down the hall, then stepped back in my doorway. "Oh, Kristy, I was thinking perhaps you could drop the package off at my place on Sunday night. It would be nice if we could go over your work together."

That invite struck at my last nerve. There was no way in hell I was going to be caught dead going to his condo just so he could hit on me in private. "I don't think so. It can wait until Monday, Tom," I bit out, praying he got the hint.

"Sunday," he said with a little more force as he stared at me. He tapped his hand on the doorframe, his eyes washing over me, and then continued on, making his way down the hall.

I reached into my bag and pulled out the USB stick that held the images I was planning to use for the layouts and placed it in the top drawer of my desk. "Guess that will just have to wait until Monday now." I giggled to myself, flipping my bag over my shoulder.

Horns blared as I stepped out onto the sidewalk. The Friday afternoon traffic is heavy already, I thought to myself as I began to walk towards home. I was about halfway down the block when snow started to fall heavily. I stopped at the grocery store just like I did every Friday for my usual bottles of wine and some snack food and wished that I had decided to drive this morning instead of walk.

"Hey, Dena." I waved at my favorite cashier as I wiped my snow-covered shoes on the mat inside the door.

"Hey, Kristy, I have already bagged your usual bottles of wine. I have them behind the counter here waiting for you. One bottle is cold, two are warm."

I nodded my thanks and made my way down the aisles to the hot food table. Had I really become that predictable that the cashier at my neighborhood Food Mart knew what wine I normally bought and had it pre-bagged for me before I'd even gotten there? I picked up some food off the hot counter, a couple of bags of chips and some candy, and made my way to the front of the store with my arms full.

Twenty minutes later, I shoved the key in the lock to my apartment and kicked the door open, running to the small table in the corner of the kitchen where I set the bags down just before they slipped out of my hands. I shoved the cold bottle of wine into the fridge, locked my apartment door, and went and had a quick shower.

Dressed in my favorite pair of yoga pants and a T-shirt, I swept my long, dark hair up into a clip and grabbed the phone. I dialed Addie's number. It was my usual Friday night bitch session where I complained to her about Tom and all the other things that had gone wrong in my life during the week.

The phone only rang once before she picked it up. "Kristy! Happy Friday!"

I laughed out loud at her enthusiasm. "Hey!" I tried but my voice clearly didn't share her sentiments.

"What's wrong? You should be thrilled to be out of that place." She giggled.

"I am just so done. Tom actually had the nerve to invite me over to his place Sunday night."

"What for?"

"He claims it was to go over my photo choices for the magazine layout. I know he is just using it as an excuse to get me alone. It pissed me off so much I may have accidentally left the USB stick that contained the images in my desk drawer. Whoops."

"You should have reported him when you had the chance. I can't believe that he's still bothering you."

"I know I should have. I just seriously need a new life. If that wasn't bad enough, he called an emergency meeting at three o'clock this afternoon to go over everything that seriously could have been summed up in an email about a paragraph long."

"What a dick."

"Then, as if everything wasn't ending on a high enough note, I stopped at Food Mart on my way home and Dena already had my three bottles of wine bagged and behind the counter. Can you believe it?"

Addie let out a loud laugh. "Oh, Kristy, that's hilarious."

"Yah it's really funny. It's pitiful. Seriously, I am twenty-five. When did I become predictable? I am supposed to be carefree, partying it up every weekend, sleeping with random dudes. Instead, the cashier at the grocery store knows that every Friday, at exactly five fifteen, I walk in and buy three bottles of Cupcake Vineyards Moscato, one cold, and two warm, to drown my sorrows over the weekend."

"It sounds like you need a vacation."

"I so do. I need away from everything," I bit out, opening the bag of gummy bears I had bought and shoving four of them in my mouth.

"Why don't you head up to the cottage? Phil and I were

supposed to go this weekend, but he's on call, so we had to change our plans."

"I don't know. It's already almost six. It would take me a bit to get there."

"Nonsense. You need this. It's supposed to be a beautiful weekend. Serenity Lake is already covered in snow, and you will have the entire cabin to yourself. You, nature, the mountains. Book a massage, go horseback riding, spend the day in nature. It's exactly what you need."

I glanced around at my empty apartment. I could either stay here and wallow in self pity, looking at the four white walls, or I could get in my car, drive up to the mountains, and spend the weekend in that beautiful rustic cabin that Addie's family had owned for years, surrounded by wildlife and beautiful scenery.

"Are you sure? I feel kind of bad going when I know you guys were planning this weekend for so long."

"I wouldn't have offered it if I wasn't sure, Kristy. Phil can't go far. His rotation was changed, and he is on call all weekend. So go, have a good time. I'll even call ahead and book you in for a massage at the hotel down the road with Shawn. I'll book it for when you arrive tonight."

"Shawn?"

"Oh you will love him. He has the best hands in the world, not to mention he is a total hottie."

I let out a laugh. I could practically see the expression on Addie's face right now as she said those words. The idea of being pampered did sound great. At least it was better than staying here and wallowing the entire weekend. "All right, fine, no need to twist my arm. I will go."

"Yay!" I could hear her clapping on the other end of the phone and imagined her jumping up and down with excitement because I'd agreed to take her up on her offer.

"Okay I am going to go and book your massage. My treat, okay! Did you want me to email you directions?"

"No, Addie, the cottage is enough. I will pay for my massage. I think I remember how to get there, but just in case I don't, please email them."

"You got it, babe! Have a great time!"

"You too."

"Oh, and don't do anything I wouldn't do." Addie laughed into the phone, and suddenly, I wished that she was joining me on this weekend away. I desperately needed girl time or something to take my mind off of everything I had going on.

We said our good-byes, and I took off down the hall towards my bedroom and packed my bag. I was going to spend the entire weekend in the mountains alone, which may be exactly what I needed to unwind.

2

Austin

I LAY with my arm over my eyes, my head pounding. It had been a long day, and I was looking forward to my days off to just lounge around the house and relax. I could hear Addie pacing outside of my bedroom door.

I glanced at the clock on the bedside table and saw it was almost six. She should have been gone on her way up to the cottage by now. I was looking forward to having the house to myself this weekend after the set of shifts I'd just had. I'd only completed two rotations after being off for an entire year and a half. I was tired, and I was seriously beginning to wonder if I hadn't jumped at the chance to go back too soon. I also wondered if perhaps it was time I found my own place. Living with my sister had its perks, but it also had its downfalls, one being zero privacy. How would I ever start dating again if she was always around nosing into everything?

Running my hand over my face, I closed my eyes and did my best to try and forget today. We'd been hanging at the fire station when the call had come in. An accident over off Jackson Street. We'd scrambled to get ready, and then, with sirens blaring, we drove like mad fools to get there. I could feel my heart in my throat as we drove there. It was the first call I'd gone on since that night.

"Austin, you doing okay?" Greg asked from the seat beside me.

"Yeah, man, all good," I lied. Memories of Jackson Street stood boldly in my mind. I knew that street all too well and did my best to avoid it at all costs.

"You're sure?"

I blew out a breath. I knew he was only asking because he cared and probably because he could tell I was stressing. "Yep all good," I lied. I could feel the adrenaline pumping through my veins.

Greg slapped me on the shoulder and called out to one of the other guys.

I looked out the front window of the rig as we slowed and that was when I saw the car, flipped upside down. My heartbeat accelerated as the rig came to a stop and the guys started climbing out. I sat there for a moment, swallowing hard, panic rising in me as I looked at the red car.

"Austin, grab the AED," I heard Greg yell.

Another surge of adrenaline, and I grabbed the AED and threw it down to Greg and climbed out of the truck. The guys rushed to a body that lay motionless on the pavement. I stood back surveying the scene, and that was when I saw an arm crushed between the pavement and the roof of the flipped car.

"Over here," I called, and two of the guys came running. "Someone is trapped." Paramedics and police arrived just as I was approaching the car. There was blood everywhere on the pavement, and I froze. I could hear a female voice weakly begging for help, bringing back all those horrible memories I had fought so hard to forget.

I froze, unable to move as panic rose in me. I could hear the guys calling me, asking me for help as they tried to lift the car to free the person inside, but I couldn't move. I just stood there, remembering.

The floor in the hallway creaked again and pulled me out of my memory. I rolled my eyes. "Why don't you just come in, Addie," I called.

My bedroom door opened, and Addie stuck her head into my room. "Oh, you're home! I didn't know you had come back from the firehouse already."

Yep, it is definitely time for me to find my own place, I thought to myself. I'd been living with my sister for the past year and a half, ever since Laura had died. I'd never even returned to our home. Addie along with her boyfriend, Phil, and Kristy, had done everything to get the house on the market, while I spent my time battling my own inner demons. I was ready to move on with my life and get over everything that had happened.

"Yep, I'm here, all six foot two, two hundred and thirty pounds of me," I murmured and then put my head back down on the pillow, covering my eyes with my arm.

"How was your day? You look spent."

"It was a day, Addie, that's all, and yes, I am tired."

"Isn't this your weekend off? You got any plans for this weekend?" she asked, plopping herself down on the end of my bed.

I stared up at the ceiling. "It is my weekend off, yes, and you have no need to worry. I won't bother you in the slightest. I plan on sleeping my entire weekend away. Besides, you aren't even going to be here, so I don't see how I will be any bother to you at all. Isn't this the weekend that you and Phil are heading up to the cottage?" I asked, silently praying that I was for sure going to have the house to myself.

Addie leaned against the wall and shook her head. "No. Unfortunately, Phil's rotation was changed, and now he is on call at the hospital, so we have to stay here."

"I see. Well, I promise you won't even know I am here." I closed my eyes and placed my arm back over them, blocking out the light to try and rid myself of the horrible headache I had.

"Austin."

I blew out a deep breath. "Yeah?"

"I hate to ask, but would it be okay if you were to head

to the cottage this weekend? I mean, you could use the quiet. You say you need the rest."

"Addie, please, I am good right here." It was clear that getting some rest right now wasn't going to happen, so I propped a pillow up behind my head and looked at my sister.

"I know. It's just... I thought maybe you could use some time in nature. It may help you reset."

"It may, but seriously, I am good here. I have food, a TV, there are a few movie marathons on this weekend. So, I'm going to nurse this headache, and then I'm just gonna chill."

Addie sat there looking at me as if she didn't want to say what was on her mind. She was up to something. I just wished she would come out and say it instead of dancing around the subject.

"Why are you trying to get rid of me?" I questioned.

"Well, I told Phil he could stay here for the weekend. It's closer to the hospital than his place. We had been planning a romantic weekend together, and it's been ruined, so I figured I'd just bring it here. I guess I just didn't think you would want to be here when..."

"All right," I said, holding my hands up for her to stop. "No need to continue. I'll get out," I said, sitting up and winking at my sister. I certainly didn't want to be here to listen to the goings on of their bedroom life, which led me again to start thinking that it was time I got my own place. There'd be no way in hell I would be able to bring a girl here, not with her bedroom butting up against mine.

The phone rang, and Addie tore off down the hall, while I got up and grabbed a duffel bag from the closet and began to pack my clothes. Forty-five minutes later, I emerged from my bedroom freshly showered, dressed in jeans and a button-down white flannel shirt. It would probably take me a good hour to get there with the weather outside, and I wanted to get on the road.

I walked into the kitchen and found Addie placing the last of the food into a cooler. "What's all this?" I opened the cupboard where we kept the first-aid kit and shook two headache tablets into my hand, popped them in my mouth, and downed a glass of water.

"I made you a care package. Figured since I am the one kicking you out, the least I could do was make sure you had food for the weekend. You've got everything you are going to need. Dinner tonight, breakfast items, stuff for lunch. I even put your favorite beer in there," she said, grinning at me. "Oh and a bottle of this." She held up a bottle.

"Thanks, but you didn't need to go to any trouble. I could just eat down at the main lodge, or better yet go to that little breakfast place in that little town that I used to love," I mumbled as I pulled out the bottle she had packed and read the name. Cupcake Vineyards Moscato.

"Oh, the one Laura never wanted to go to?" Addie said nonchalantly.

I frowned, not saying anything as I put the bottle back into the box.

"What is it?" she asked.

"Nothing. Nothing at all." I'd asked Addie numerous times to never to mention Laura to me. I knew it had been a slip of the tongue, and I didn't want to make her feel bad, so I just let the comment slide.

"Well, here you go," she said, pushing the box towards me. "Just drive careful, and I will see you on Monday."

"Yep." I grabbed the cooler and box of food, threw my duffel bag over my shoulder, and walked down the back porch to my car.

3

Kristy

MUSIC BLARED over the radio as I drove up the road to the entrance of Serenity Lake. I still couldn't believe that Addie had just offered me the entire weekend up at the cottage. I knew she and Phil had been planning this weekend for a while. It was their anniversary, and part of me felt guilty for accepting it, even though I knew she couldn't attend.

I slowed down as I approached the entrance to a newly built hotel on Serenity Lake. My stomach flipped with excitement. The place had changed a lot since I had been there last. I pulled the car in front of the hotel and cut the engine. I looked up at the stone building. I remembered coming up here to the cottage with Addie's family when we were younger, long before this hotel was built. I remembered seeing all the Christmas lights that each cottage owner had strung around their properties, some adjoining them together through the trees and around the lake. I looked around and the same feeling presented itself. I glanced off to the left where a huge bonfire was burning. People were scattered around the fire, relaxing on Adirondack chairs.

I climbed out of the car, locked the doors, and approached the front door to the main lodge. There was a long line of people waiting to be checked in at the front desk. I glanced around. Not only was it beautiful in here but cozy too. Couples sat in large, over-sized leather chairs around a huge stone fireplace. It would be a perfect place to read the book I brought, I thought to myself.

I glanced at my watch. I knew Addie had booked me an appointment at the spa, and if I waited in this line to check in for my appointment, I would be late. I glanced around the lobby and spotted the sign for Serenity Cove and headed in that direction.

I was welcomed at the desk with a glass of cucumber water and led to the changing room where I slipped into a plush white bathrobe, monogrammed with SC on the pocket. I was then directed to go and relax in a beautiful solarium with a view of the lake. I had barely sat down in the reclining chair when I was brought a hot chamomile tea. The view of the snow-covered landscape combined with the music and warm tea had me fully relaxed from my drive by the time Shawn had come to get me. Addie had been right. He was extremely easy on the eyes, I thought as I followed him down the hall to his treatment room.

I lay on the massage table with my eyes closed, while Shawn massaged all the tension away from my back and shoulders, digging into every knotted muscle he could find. Addie hadn't been lying when she mentioned he had amazing hands. He spent time working on every aching muscle in my body, and I felt like Jell-O when he was finished. He left the room, and I lay on the table in the dim light for a few minutes, allowing myself to come back down.

Feeling refreshed and relaxed, I left the spa and went out to my car. I started heading down the road towards the cottage and spotted a restaurant off to my left. I pulled in and smiled. The Country Winds Pub was still here. I shut the car off and headed inside. Once seated, I placed an order for a hamburger and fries to go. I was eager just to get to the cottage and continue relaxing with some food and a bottle of wine.

Another twenty minutes down the road, I finally approached the cabin. It was tucked away on the opposite side of the lake from that new hotel and was nestled back in off the road surrounded by trees. It was a cute rustic cabin from the outside, and I hurried to grab my bag, food, and make my way inside. I pushed the door open and glanced inside. It looked exactly how I remembered it. I set my food on the table and took my bag into the bedroom, placing it on the king-sized bed, and sat down to test out the soft mattress. I was looking forward to sinking my body into it tonight.

I looked around the room and saw a tray on the bedside table I hadn't noticed when I first walked in. A little A-frame card with the words "Our Compliments" written on it. I knew Addie owned part of this time-share and wondered if the hotel staff was the ones who looked after it. I sat up and sifted through the items that were in the basket. I picked up a purple box and opened it, sliding out a sealed bag.

"The Womanizer," I read out loud. "30 mins worth of pleasure. This could come in useful," I said, giggling before throwing it down on the table and moving to the next box. I opened it and a bottle of lavender-scented massage oil fell into my hands. The next box contained a bottle of warming lubricant, and the last box contained ten condoms. Too bad I wouldn't be needing these this weekend, I thought, piling everything back into the basket. Addie had a bit of a dirty side to her, I chuckled to myself. Bet she forgot that she had requested these be here.

I wandered back into the living room, turned on the gas fireplace that was across from the couch, and flipped on the TV for some background noise. The little kitchenette had everything I would need for the weekend, I thought as I opened the cupboards, seeing they were fully stocked with dishes. I poked my head into the last room and spotted a huge Jacuzzi tub, something I definitely planned on climbing into before the weekend was over. My apartment only had a shower, so it was rare I got to soak in a tub of hot water. I slipped my shoes off and sank my socked feet into the plush carpet and opened a window just a crack to air the place out.

Pulling a wine glass from the cupboard, I went in search of the bottles of wine I had shoved into my bag of clothes. Grabbing all three, I placed two of them into the cold fridge and opened one, pouring myself a glass. I had just spread the spare blanket that rested on the back of the couch on the floor and slid the coffee table out of the way. Then I placed my burger and fries into the microwave and set it to reheat.

I went into the bedroom and quickly changed out of my clothes and into a T-shirt and panties. I had nothing to do tonight now but relax, I thought as I pulled my food from the microwave, took it into the living room, and plunked down onto the floor.

After I ate, I dialed Addie's number. I wanted her to know I had arrived safely and thank her for the wonderful massage. Her phone rang several times. I was just about to hang up when she answered.

"Hey."

"Hey. Everything okay?" she questioned. I should have known she would be worried, since I didn't call her when I first arrived as promised.

"Yep, I just wanted to let you know I made it, and I am safe."

"Oh great. How was Shawn?"

"My God, you were so right. He has AMAZING hands. When did they build that gorgeous hotel?" I lay down on the floor and stared up at the ceiling.

"About eight months ago. Beautiful isn't it. I am so glad you are all relaxed."

"I am. I completely forgot what it felt like to be completely relaxed. My body feels like Jell-O." I giggled.

"It's amazing isn't it."

"It so is. I even stopped in at the Country Winds Pub. I was so surprised it was still there."

"Yep, still there and as good as ever."

"Oh, and it was very thoughtful of you to leave me the welcome basket in the bedroom. It really is too bad that I don't have anyone to share it with."

I heard Addie gasp and did my best not to laugh out loud.

"Oh my God, I am so embarrassed. I forgot all about it," Addie cried into the phone. "Don't mention anything to Phil. It was supposed to be a surprise."

All I could do was laugh. At first, it had been embarrassing finding it, but now that I'd had wine and could hear Addie's reaction, it was just funny.

"Adding a little kink into the bedroom, were you, Addie?" I blushed at my own comment.

Addie let out a laugh. "How much wine have you had?"

"Just a bottle or so. I'm fine."

"All right, well, you enjoy your night. I'm glad you got there safely."

"You enjoy your night too. Although I am the one with the basket of goodies." I hiccupped. "Oh, and don't do anything I wouldn't do with Phil." As soon as the words left my lips, I knew that wasn't how I meant them to come out. "I mean, not what I would do with Phil. Just anything I wouldn't do with him." I giggled and was surprised when I hiccupped again, which caused me to laugh even more.

"Oh my, you enjoy your wine, Kristy." Addie let out a laugh. "You might want to stop soon."

"I will. Oh where can I get some groceries? I will need food."

"There is a little grocer about a five-minute drive from the entrance to the hotel. Go tomorrow," Addie said.

"I plan on it. I'm not going anywhere tonight. I have no pants on. They probably have one of those signs: no pants no service." I giggled.

"Oh my God, girl, get a grip on yourself." Addie laughed. "You need to get away more often."

"Addie."

"Yes."

"You know what I need?"

"Dare I ask?"

"What I need is a big strapping man to take care of all my troubles. That is what I need. A man who isn't afraid to pound me into the mattress. A man who won't sink his tongue into another woman when I am five floors below him," I said as I ran my finger around the rim of the wine glass that sat on the table in front of me, tears coming to my eyes. "You know, someone who makes me feel like a woman and treats me the way I am supposed to be treated."

"I swear, if you break out in song right now, I'm hanging up."

I heard Phil in the background calling to Addie. "Guess I'll let you go. Have fun."

"I'll talk to you Monday." We said our good-byes and hung up.

I poured myself another glass of wine, emptying the bottle into my glass. I wiped away the stray tears and reached behind me, grabbing the pillows off the couch, situating them perfectly behind me and curling one under my head. I got up and locked the door, shutting the window I had opened, and grabbed the other spare blanket from the bed. I lay down on the floor and covered myself up and began watching TV.

4

Austin

I stopped at the light just on the outskirts of our neigh-borhood. The second the light turned green, and I pulled through the intersection and turned into the parking lot of the local coffee shop. If I was going to make this drive tonight, I was going to need a jolt of caffeine to wake me up.

It only took a couple of minutes before a large, hot coffee sat in the cup holder and I was pulling back out onto the snow-covered street. I wondered what had caused Addie to hand over the cottage for the weekend. She and Phil had been planning this trip for months now and had to book the time-share almost a year in advance. She had begged him to wait until winter as she'd always wanted to spend time up in the mountains with snow on the ground. I really hoped I hadn't somehow upset her and that she was telling me the truth when she had said that he was on call for the weekend. I hoped that I hadn't overstayed my welcome. Eighteen months was a long time to live with your brother. Truthfully, I had been there longer than I had even originally planned, but how was I supposed to know how long it would take me to get over everything that had happened?

I was driving through town heading towards the highway when the car in front of me jammed on their brakes. I swore under my breath and broke hard, my tires sliding. I did everything I could to avoid hitting the backend of their car. As we started up again, a funny feeling came over me. I was at the intersection of Jackson and Mackenzie. The dreaded intersection that I had managed to avoid for the entire year and a half, until today. Today, I had somehow managed to be here twice.

While I sat waiting for the light to change, my mind floated to that dreaded night that had been permanently ingrained into my memory.

I was at the station, packing up my bag, getting ready for the end of my four-day stint. I was excited to be heading home, looking forward to spending time with my wife, when a call came over the radio. I glanced at the clock. It was ten. Another couple of hours and we would be in the clear. Instead, the bell rang out. I dropped everything, and we all got suited up and piled into the truck.

"There's been an accident at the intersection of Jackson and Mackenzie. Sounds to be head-on, one car flipped, one

person pinned in their car. Unknown injuries. Probable drunk driver," Greg said as we loaded into the big rig.

With sirens blaring, the truck raced across the city. Minutes later, we were there, and the guys unloaded one by one. Since I had been one of the first on the truck at the station, I was one of the last guys off the truck. I had just put my foot on the pavement when I heard our captain yell something about "get him back in the truck." I turned around just as Greg made his way over to me, and my heart literally stopped at the scene in front of me.

"Austin, come on, man, get back in the truck," Greg said, fighting to try and force me to turn around. "You don't need to see this."

"Laura...No, no, no, no," was all I could get out before I lunged onto the scene, pushing Greg out of the way. I ran in the direction of the blue Mazda that was wrapped around a pole.

Greg tried again to stop me, grabbing at my coat, two of the other guys grabbing me by the arms, but I pushed through them all. "Let him go," I heard the captain say from behind me.

I ran to the car. There in the front seat with her head resting against the steering wheel was my wife, Laura. The airbag hadn't deployed. The second I put my hand on her, she opened her eyes. I could tell she didn't know where she was. Her gaze was one I'll never forget. She looked at me, murmuring, "I'm sorry."

A horn blaring from behind pulled me out of my

memory and I glanced up, noticing the light had turned green. Not knowing how long I had been sitting there, I swallowed hard and accelerated through the intersection, pulling onto the highway. I took a sip of my hot coffee, turned up the radio, and focused on the road ahead, but soon that memory overtook me again.

I wanted her out of that car. I had to get her out of that car. I pulled on the door, but it wouldn't budge. Instead, I knelt at the side of her mangled car, reached in, and brushed away her blood-soaked hair from her face, trying to keep her calm, while the guys did their best to figure out how they were going to get her out. All she kept mumbling to me was, "I'm sorry." I had no idea what she meant by that, and at the moment I didn't care. I just sat there doing my best not to lose my shit while I tried to comfort her.

Seven days later, I buried my wife. I remembered it clear as day. I had wanted to go home after the funeral, but Addie said I needed to be at the celebration of life. I was with Addie, Phil, and Kristy, and a bunch of guys from the firehouse when Laura's best friend Kelley had walked in. She made her rounds before approaching me, her eyes filling with tears as she hugged me, sharing her condolences.

"I'm so sorry about Laura," she'd said.

I could still hear Laura's words in my mind, "I'm sorry," for whatever reason. I'd be haunted forever by those words, and I hadn't even known what they meant.

"Thank you," I said, my sister coming to my side to hand me a glass of water.

"I told her not to go, you know. I told her you were the best thing that had ever happened to her, but she did it anyways," Kelley said.

I frowned. "What do you mean? You told her not to go where?" I questioned as I stared at Kelley. I felt Addie's hand on my arm, but I shrugged out of it. Laura and I had been having relationship issues for the past couple of years. Things hadn't been good, but we had been working on it. We'd gotten in to see one of the best marriage counselors in our area, and he had said that with work we could fix us. We had promised one another that we would work on us.

"She went to Scott's the night before," Kelley said almost like it didn't matter, or perhaps like she thought I knew.

I glanced across the room at where Laura's ex sat, while Kelley continued rambling on. He had recently moved back into town, and they had connected one day at a coffee shop. She claimed that they were friends. I never really thought anything of it. I watched him while he sat there laughing it up with some friends. He must have felt me watching him because he glanced over at me, giving me a look of pity.

Suddenly, a darkness that scared even me came over me. Addie and Kristy both stepped in between Kelley and me, sending her away. I didn't need to hear it from someone else. I now knew what the words "I'm sorry" had meant.

She'd been having an affair with the man who sat three tables away from me. I knew our marriage was on the rocks, but for her to actually go through with it...

Another car horn blared from behind and I glanced up, almost missing the cut-off for Serenity Lake. Perhaps this weekend will do me good, I thought to myself as I pushed the memory of that day out of my mind.

I passed by the newly built hotel and continued on down the road when I saw the Country Winds Pub. My stomach let out a loud growl, so I pulled in and parked the car. The second I climbed out of the truck, I could already smell the clean mountain air. It was peaceful, the sounds of the city left far behind.

I pulled the door open and entered the quiet pub. A few people sat at tables, but the bar was empty. I glanced at my watch. It was only nine, and honestly, anything with alcohol sounded good right about now. I walked on over to the bar and took a seat, looking at the menu.

"Evening. Can I get you something to drink?"

I glanced at the nametag on his shirt: Jesse. "Sure, Jesse. I'll take a beer," I said.

"Did you want to try our own. It's our Serene Pale Ale."

"Sure, why not."

While Jesse poured me a beer and took my order, I quickly sent off a message to Addie letting her know I had arrived and was just grabbing a bite to eat before heading to the cabin. While I sat there drinking down the cold beverage, I watched as a group of women came walking in and sat down at a table in the corner. They were loud and giggling and I smiled to myself when their drinks were delivered. They broke out in a toast to one of the girls.

"You staying at the lake, sir?" Jesse asked as he set another full glass down on the bar in front of me, taking away my already empty glass. The first one went down way too fast, I thought to myself.

"Yeah, up here for the weekend. A little R&R."

"Well, you picked the right place. Where are you staying? Main hotel?"

"No, my sister and I own a time-share not too far down the road, right on the lake."

"Those are beautiful cabins. Is your wife or girlfriend already there?"

"Nope, it's just me," I bit out, not really wanting to carry on that part of the conversation. "My sister couldn't make it with her boyfriend this weekend, so she offered it to me."

"That was nice. Well, it's a fair walk, but the hiking trail starts at the end of the road and goes right around the lake. I highly suggest taking a walk through the trail. Snow is a little deep right now, but you can rent snowshoes at the hotel or at the ski hills."

"Sounds good."

"There are some hot girls here this week staying in some of the cabins," he said, nodding to the group of women in the corner.

I nodded, glanced over at the women, and raised my

glass to the bartender to order one more beer. Jesse flipped the TV on behind the bar for me, brought me my food and another beer, and set the bill on the counter in front of me. I had just finished my last bite and threw some cash down when another group of about twenty or so walked in.

The tiny pub got louder, and my quiet little haven was soon blaring music so loud I could barely think. I drank down the last little bit of the beer I'd been nursing and waved a thanks to Jesse and headed out to my truck.

It was snowing much harder now as I made my way up the road to the cottage. I had to slow down to find the end of the driveway. I pulled my car in only to notice another vehicle was already parked there. I frowned. Perhaps I had the wrong cottage. I checked again, feeling rather irritated that somehow the cottage had already been rented out to someone else. Perhaps Addie had the wrong weekend, I thought. I was just about to pick up my cell phone when I caught sight of the Tweety Bird decal on the back wind-shield of the car that was parked in front of me. That was Kristy's car. I'd know it anywhere because I had been the one who put the decal on. It had been a gift from Addie for Kristy's twenty-third birthday, and as soon as she opened it and saw it, she had pleaded with me to put it on.

"What the hell is Kristy doing here?" I mumbled to myself as I opened the truck, grabbing my duffel bag, cooler, and box of food. There was no way that she would come up here without Addie's permission. Which made me wonder what my sister was up to.

I made my way up to the front door of the cabin. I could see a light on inside, and I cautiously opened the door. I was immediately hit with a wave of heat. It had to be almost ninety degrees in the room. I pushed the door open and stepped inside, letting the cool air into the cabin.

I set my things on the floor just inside the door and stepped into the front room, removing my coat and placing my keys on the table. I glanced into the living room, and there, sprawled out on a blanket in the middle of the floor, was Kristy. No wonder she hadn't asked who was here. Two empty bottles of wine lay over on their sides on the carpet, half of a glass of wine sat on the table. She rolled over and the blanket fell away, exposing her. She lay there in a short T-shirt, her tiny ass framed by purple cotton panties. I chuckled to myself at the sight.

I took my shoes off, wiped the sweat from my brow, and shut the fireplace off before walking over to where she slept on the floor. She couldn't stay on the floor all night.

I went into the bedroom that was just off the living room and pulled down the covers on the king-sized bed. Then I went back and scooped her up off the floor and into my arms. Her head fell against my chest, and she murmured something in her sleep that I couldn't understand. I looked down at her, her cheek resting against my chest as I carried her into the bedroom. I lay her down gently and pulled the covers over her. She softly mumbled something else that was completely incoherent and fell back into a deep sleep.

I shut the bedroom door and then cracked open a window and removed my shirt before unpacking the cooler that Addie had sent with me. Then I picked up the blankets off the floor and looked around. I had forgotten that the cabin only had one bedroom. If I was going to stay here, I would need a place to sleep. I checked the couch and realized that it was a futon and laid it out flat. I flicked the button open on my jeans and let them drop to the floor. Now I stood in my boxers trying to figure out how the hell I was going to fit on this futon.

First, I lay down on my back, hanging my legs over the railings, thinking it might not be that bad. After a few minutes, I could feel the circulation in my legs dulling. Several more minutes later, I had shifted and tried lying diagonally across it, only to be annoyed that half my legs lay off the mattress. Finally, in a huff, I threw the blanket off me and got up.

Fuck it, I thought and headed for the bedroom. "We are friends and two grown adults," I whispered to myself. "Surely, she won't mind sharing the bed with me for one night." I grabbed my duffel bag and pulled my grey sweatpants out for the morning.

I opened the door slowly and approached the bed, laying my sweatpants on the chair that sat in the corner on my way past. I pulled the covers down and eased myself onto the mattress, careful not to disturb her. My body instantly sank into the soft mattress. I lay there staring up at the ceiling, Kristy sound asleep beside me, and started laughing to myself. This was so not the way I'd ever imagined myself sharing a bed with her. Of course, out of all the years I had known her, I never ever should have thought about sharing a bed with Kristy to begin with. Not only was she Addie's best friend, but I should have thought of her more as a sister than anything else, but my body and surging hormones had other ideas.

I closed my eyes, my mind wandering to the purple panties she was wearing, and I looked over to the side of her bed. The moonlight coming through the window was enough to outline the soft curve of her hip. I felt my cock start to stir, and I covered it with my palm to try to stop the raging hard-on that was forming. It had been years, and I was sure I was over thinking of her this way. My body, however, let me know that I was not.

5

Kristy

I opened my eyes, blinking more than once, trying to clear my blurry vision. My mouth was dry and my head was pounding. That's what I get for drinking two bottles of wine, I thought to myself. I didn't recognize the wall I was looking at, and I had to think hard about where I was. I rubbed my arm. I was freezing, and I reached for the blankets to cover myself up. I had just closed my eyes when I remembered I was up at the cottage. The last thing I remembered was lying on the floor, watching TV while drinking wine. Why couldn't I remember crawling into bed?

I rolled over onto my side and saw someone lying beside me, his hand over his face as he gently snored. I thought nothing of it and laid my head on my pillow and closed my eyes, but then the realization hit. Who the hell was in bed with me? I pulled the covers over my head quickly and then ever so slowly poked my head out to look and see if I could tell who it was that was lying beside me.

I blinked a couple of times to make sure I wasn't dreaming. The blankets lay resting on his hips, those deeply carved V lines prominent against the blanket. My eyes traveled up to his solid eight-pack, then to his large, bulky chest and strong shoulders. I didn't need to see his face to know who it was. I had been dreaming of licking those lines and running my hands over his chest since my teen years. I tore my eyes away just in time for his arm to move. I bit my bottom lip as I looked up to see Austin, his eyes closed, his face relaxed.

"Are you okay? You're not going to be sick are you? If you are, there is a bowl on your side of the bed. I'd prefer you get sick in that than on me." His deep, sexy, sleepy voice filled the room.

I jumped. Oh God, he was awake. What if he'd seen me checking him out? I could feel the panic rising, but then I realized it was impossible as his arm had been covering his eyes the entire time.

"Kristy?" he questioned.

"I'm okay. What the...what are you doing here?" I asked, my voice shaking.

"I should be the one asking you that. Addie sent me away so she could get wild and dirty with Phil this weekend." He shivered at the thought.

I let out a tiny giggle at his reaction. "Addie told me I

could stay here this weekend." As I spoke the words, I realized that she must have planned this in some way.

I glanced around the room, noticing his sweatpants on the chair in the corner. I lifted the blanket to see I still had my T-shirt and panties on, and I silently thanked God. I wouldn't want to have done something with him and not remembered. "How did we end up in bed together?" I asked, my voice barely above a whisper.

Austin chuckled. "How about you come with me and I will demonstrate," he said, kicking the covers off him and getting out of bed.

As he stood, I couldn't help my eyes running over his body. They wandered from his broad shoulders down his muscular back and landed on his tight ass. I wondered what it would be like to dig my fingers into his back, then I thought that there was no way I should be having thoughts of my best friend's brother.

"Are you coming?" he asked as he got to the bedroom doorway and turned around looking back at me.

I went to kick the covers off and get up out of bed when I realized I was in the shortest T-shirt I owned. I quickly threw the covers back over me and sat there. I had no idea why I was suddenly embarrassed. Austin had seen me many times in a bathing suit, which was far less than I had on now.

"Don't be embarrassed. I already saw it all." He laughed.

I wanted to die. Who the hell knows how he found me last

night, I thought to myself. I sat there for a few more minutes, while he wandered into the living room, then I kicked the blankets off and stood up, pulling on the hem of my T-shirt to try and cover everything as I followed after him.

"See, I came in last night, you were sprawled out on the floor, completely passed out. I picked you up and put you to bed, then I unpacked my stuff. I was going to sleep out here, but this piece of garbage is...well, just that." He chuckled and laid down on the futon.

I let out a laugh as he tried lying down, his legs hanging over the end of the futon. I watched as he then moved to lie across it diagonally, and I let out another laugh at the fact that both his head and feet were off the mattress.

"Not exactly what I'd call comfort," he bit out, getting frustrated as he tried bending his large frame in a position that wouldn't be comfortable even for me.

I giggled again. I couldn't help it. He had always been cute when he got frustrated. "I guess not."

"You guess not? Did you know there is a lump right in the center? How about you lay down on this thing. See for yourself."

I shook my head, trying hard not to laugh at him, but I couldn't help it.

"You really think this is funny?" he asked, sitting up. I noticed his eyes ran the length of my body and back to my face.

A shiver ran through me. "It's freezing," I said, finally

letting go of the hem of T-shirt and crossing my arms across my chest. I glanced up and noticed the window above the couch was still open a crack.

Austin looked in the same direction. "Well, in all fairness, it was almost a hundred degrees when I got here. You fell asleep with the fireplace on. If I hadn't of shown up, you probably would have dehydrated. So, I saved your life." He stood and reached to slide the window shut. "Why don't you go crawl back into bed? I'll get dressed and go and see if that hotel has an available room, or I'll rent another cabin."

I watched as he reached to grab his jeans. A funny feeling in my stomach told me to tell him to stay, but getting the words out seemed to be a little difficult. He had slid one leg into his jeans when I finally managed to speak. "Austin, just stay here."

He stopped and turned to look in my direction, his eyes once again sweeping my body. "Are you sure?"

"Yes. I wouldn't have offered if I weren't. Plus, you and Addie are the ones who pay for the time-share slot. It would only be fair if I were the one who left, not you."

"What about sleeping arrangements?" he questioned, his eyes once again falling the length the of my body.

"It's okay. It's supposed to be cold this weekend. You can keep me warm," I said, winking. What on earth had gotten into me? Ten minutes ago I had been mortified that he was going to get a full view of me in a T-shirt and panties, and now I stood here practically hitting on the guy. No, I *was* hitting on the guy.

I smiled and turned and went and crawled back in the soft bed and covered myself up. Once in bed, I lay there and listened hard to see if I heard Austin rummaging around, packing up his stuff, but the place was silent.

A few minutes later, Austin appeared in the bedroom doorway. "I put the fireplace on," he murmured and approached the bed, pulling the covers down and slipping under them.

Our eyes locked, and the next thing I knew, he raised his arm, inviting me in for a cuddle. I scooted over and pressed myself up against his warm body, a feeling of nervousness running through me as he brought his arm down around me and rested his hand on my hip. Perhaps this wasn't going to be a shitty weekend after all.

6

Austin

I LAY IN BED, staring up at the ceiling. The sunlight was pouring through the slats of the blinds, and I glanced at my watch. I was shocked to find that it was already ten. I couldn't remember the last time I had slept that long.

I moved slightly to roll onto my side when I felt resistance and heard Kristy murmur. I looked down to see her head resting on my abdomen, her arm around my waist. I smiled to myself and put my hand on the back of her head, ruffling her hair.

"Good morning," I said, doing my best not to startle her.

"Morning," she mumbled sleepily.

"Would you like a coffee?"

"Yes please," she said as she pushed herself up into a sitting position and looked at me. She glanced down at what she had been using for her pillow, her cheeks turning a light shade of pink when she realized that it was me. "Sorry for using you as a pillow."

I couldn't help but chuckle. She was too cute. "It's okay. I didn't mind. You stay here. I will get us coffee."

I kicked the covers off and reached for my grey sweatpants in the chair and slid them on. I looked over my shoulder before I left the room. Kristy lay on her side facing me, and that was when I realized that she had been watching me dress.

With that thought in mind, I went into the kitchenette and filled the kettle and set it to boil. I rooted through the box of food Addie had sent with me and finally found the coffee buried in the bottom of the box. I would have thought she would have set it at the top.

I busied myself making coffee and then opened the fridge and pulled out the eggs and bacon I had put in there last night and began heating a pan I'd found in the cupboard.

While the bacon sizzled away in the pan, I flipped the eggs in the other pan before pouring two mugs of hot coffee and carrying them into the bedroom. Kristy was now relaxed against the pillows she had propped up behind her back and was watching TV.

"Here you go, just the way you like it." I smiled, handing her the mug. "Careful, it's hot."

"What took you so long? I feared maybe you didn't know how to make coffee." She gave a cute giggle.

"Please." I let out a laugh and returned to the kitchen where I plated the food onto two plates and carried them into the bedroom. The second I rounded the corner carrying the plates, her eyes lit up at the sight of food.

"Breakfast in bed? How did you know?"

"I knew. Besides, I was hungry, so I figured you might be as well," I said, handing her her plate and sitting down on the edge of the bed with mine so I could face her.

"You've got to be the best…" She paused for a second and looked at me and smiled. "The best not-my-boyfriend boyfriend ever."

I couldn't help but laugh. "Thanks I think," I said, biting into a piece of the crisp bacon. "Speaking of boyfriends. How's Tom?"

Immediately, she looked down at her plate and a look came across her face I wasn't sure I'd seen before. She took a sip of her coffee, set the mug down, and looked at me. "Things ended with Tom when I caught him with his face between the legs of his assistant… in his office," she said matter of fact.

I almost choked on my eggs as the words fell from her lips. "Hell, Kristy, I didn't know. I'm sorry." I didn't want her to think I was being an insensitive prick.

"No, it's okay. I know you didn't know. I'd told Addie, but I asked her not to say anything to anyone. It was embarrassing enough to have my entire office know before I did."

"Oh, trust me, I get it."

"It's just now he thinks because he is the boss he can hold all kinds of things over my head. I guess I should have reported him when I had the chance."

"Honestly, I never liked the guy. He always struck me as being a power-hungry little ass," I bit out.

Kristy laughed. "Yes, that he is. I'd forgotten you'd met him."

"Well, between you and I, I always thought you could do better," I said absentmindedly while dipping my toast into my egg yolk.

Kristy was bringing her toast to her mouth when she stopped and looked at me. "You did?"

"Yep, to be honest, I've never liked any of the guys you've dated. I'll tell you I only tolerated Tom because Addie had begged me to. There were plenty of times I should have taken him out back and taught him a lesson."

"Oh," she said, biting into her toast.

We both grew quiet. I wasn't sure if I wanted to divulge why or not, because it would only bring up memories I didn't want to revisit this weekend. However, she sat there looking at me, and I knew she was wondering why, so once I had swallowed what was in my mouth, I decided not to hold back.

"Do you remember when you brought him to Addie's Fourth of July party?"

"Yeah."

"Did you know that he hit on Laura when she was coming back from the bathroom?" I asked.

"Addie never told me that!"

"She wouldn't have because she didn't know. I never told her, but you can be rest assured I knew about it, and the only thing keeping me from dragging his ass outside was the fact that Laura begged me not to make a scene."

"Was that right before dinner?"

"Yep."

"What did you say? I remember he came to me just as Addie and I were pulling stuff from the kitchen and demanded to go home."

Kristy sat there wide-eyed waiting for me to say something. I finished chewing what was in my mouth, took a sip of coffee, and smiled to myself. "Let's put it this way, what I said to him was not meant for a lady's ears."

Kristy met my eyes. I could tell she didn't know what to say. Then she smiled. "I'm sorry about him."

"Don't be, it's in the past. Truth be known, she probably instigated the entire thing herself, and I tore a strip off an innocent guy who was caught in the wrong place at the wrong time."

"Don't say that," Kristy said, reaching out and touching my hand. "She loved you."

I grew quiet. I didn't know what to think of those words, especially coming from Kristy. I wasn't sure that Laura had ever loved me at all.

"Yep, perhaps at one time she might have, but that, too,

is in the past now." Kristy knew all about what had transpired at the funeral home. She had been the one who had taken me outside while the guys from the fire department had asked Scott to leave. She had been the one who stayed with me while I lost my shit out in the back alley, and she had also been the one whose arms held me while I'd cried my heart out. She'd seen it all, and because of that, we had grown closer in a much different way.

"You finished?" I said, nodding at her empty plate and winking at her, trying to change the subject.

"Yes," she said, handing me the plate. "It was really good."

"I'm glad you enjoyed it." I took the plates and dropped them into the sink in the kitchen, then wandered back into the bedroom and sat back down, propping my pillow up behind my back and sitting beside Kristie.

"What do you want to do today?" I asked.

"Well, honestly, I could just relax in bed all day, cuddle, and watch TV. Although, I think perhaps we could go for a hike instead, get some fresh air. Maybe grab some groceries before that so we have something good for dinner."

"That sounds like a plan."

We took our time getting ready, both of us taking a hot shower, and then we piled into his truck.

7

Kristy

On our way back from the grocery store, we stopped in at a little local snowshoe rental shack. Austin hopped out and grabbed us both a pair and got a trail map of the area. We stopped back into the cottage to put away the groceries and get changed into something a little warmer.

It had only taken us a couple of hours, but we had hiked the entire trail around the lake. Neither of us had been here in years—basically since we were kids. I remembered coming up here in the summer with Addie's family and going to the lake with her and Austin. We'd swim and fish, but as I got older, I developed a crush on Austin. Once I had hit sixteen, I would find myself coming up with excuses as to why I could no longer go with them on family vacations.

We had just returned from returning the snowshoes to the little rental hut and parked the truck next to the cabin.

"Did you want to head down to the lake?" Austin questioned, coming around from the driver's side and walking beside me.

I looked out at the lake. There were families out there building snowmen and snow forts. "Sure, that sounds great." I smiled.

We headed off in the direction of the lake and soon were out on the familiar dock that still housed the colorful Adirondack chairs for people to sit on.

"I'm surprised the lake hasn't frozen over yet," I said, brushing the snow off one of the chairs and sitting down.

"Even though it's colder than normal this year, it hasn't been cold enough to freeze the water just yet," Austin said, picking up a rock and skipping it across the water.

I sat there and watched in amazement as the rock went flying across the water's surface. "I still have no idea how you do that."

"What? Skip rocks? It's easy."

"Sure it is. You are telling that to someone who can't do it."

"It is easy! First, the stone should be mostly flat and about the size of the palm of your hand. If you can, try and find a triangular stone as those ones skip the best, but stay away from circular stones," Austin said, bending over and picking up another stone. He looked over at me and cocked his head. "Come over here."

"Why?"

"Just come over here. I'm gonna teach you how to do this."

I knew there was no fighting him. He would just walk over and force me out of this chair. Instead, I got up and walked over to him. He held the stone out for me to see. I peeked into his hand, but instead of showing me, he grabbed my hand and dropped the stone into mine. I examined it then held it out for him to take.

"No, no, no, you are going to do it," he said, refusing to take the stone back.

I looked at him like he was crazy. "Austin, you know I can't do this. It's only going to sink on me."

He chuckled. "How about you trust me. Now you said you wanted to learn, so let's learn."

"No, what I said was that I have no idea how you do that. I never said I wanted to learn," I said, sticking my tongue out at him.

He chucked again and then came around behind me and positioned the stone in my hand the correct way.

"So you're going to hold it with your thumb and middle finger." He positioned my fingers the way they needed to be. "Then you're going to firmly hook your index finger along the edge of the stone, your thumb on top of the stone, not around the edge."

"All right, so now what?"

He stepped up behind me and placed his hand on my lower abdomen, pulling me back against him. The second my body hit his it was like I could barely breathe. I was glad he was behind me supporting me because my knees felt a little weak.

"Okay, so now you are going to stand up straight," his deep, sexy voice echoed in my ear. With his chest pressing against my back, he turned me until I was at a slight angle to the water. "Now you're going to stay in this position during the windup and release. The lower your hand is at the release, the better. You're going to throw out and down at the same time. It needs plenty of downward force, faster not harder, and you're going to spin it hard with a quick snap of your wrist."

I was afraid to move. Every nerve in my body was going off at the fact his body was pressed against mine. I felt hot and shaky and a lot anxious, but I did the only thing I knew to do, and that was let him have full control over my movements. Next thing I knew, I was watching the stone skip across the water.

Austin stood there, his arms still wrapped around me, taking in my expression. We locked eyes and stood there in silence staring at one another. His hand went to my cheeks, his eyes moving from my eyes to my lips. I was sure he was going to kiss me, but voices in the distance caused us both to part.

"See, it's not that hard," Austin said, stepping away from me and sitting down on one of the other chairs. "Try it again. I know you can do it."

I searched through the rocks, finally finding one that

was similarly shaped, repeating everything that Austin had shown me, round up and let the rock go, only to have it drop right into the water and sink. Austin let out a laugh behind me, and I turned, pouting at him. "I told you that was what would happen."

"Come on, just give it another shot. Rome wasn't built in a day. You'll get it."

"I will never learn to do that," I said, sitting down in the chair beside him and looking out over the lake. "Do you remember how your parents used to sit here and watch us while we all swam out to the platform in the middle of lake?" I asked.

"Yep, they sat here sipping on mimosas and wine while we all went crazy cannonballing into the water."

"You were the only one who cannonballed. Addie and I just wanted to sun out on the platform. Instead, all you did was splash us."

"Yep, and I swear I only did the cannonballs to make you girls angry." Austin laughed. "It was so fun to get the two of you going."

"Do you remember that summer that Addie had a crush on that guy that was here, and he had swum out to the platform and was making small talk with her?"

"Yep."

"You remember climbing out of the water, seeing it, and running towards her, grabbing her, and jumping into the water? She was so angry with you."

"Yeah, it was hilarious. The guy was a dog though. I'd

caught him down at the beach earlier that morning before you girls were up. He had walked up behind this woman who was setting out her blanket and he pulled the tie on the back of her bikini. I'll admit, she had nice ones, but it was a shitty thing to do. I didn't want my sister hanging around with that ass, so as mad as she got, it was worth it. I probably saved her from a relationship of regret."

"I had no idea Addie was so angry at you. She went on about that for weeks you know. If I probably brought it up today, she would still go on about it."

"Yeah, I know. I got it from Dad later that night." Austin chuckled at the memory.

"By this time then, your parents would have been well into the booze. It's clearly not too early to start is it?"

"Nope. I'll be right back." Austin stood, picking up another rock and making it look completely effortless as he sent it skipping across the lake again.

"You suck!" I giggled. Austin turned and smiled at me and started walking up towards the cabin. "Where are you going?"

"You'll see."

I wrapped my coat around me a little tighter as a cold breeze came off the lake. I relaxed back against the chair and watched the birds float through the trees and listened to the sounds of nature. All the memories from when we were kids ran through my mind so vividly. It was almost as if I were sitting here watching them all play out in front of me. I was so deeply focused on my thoughts that I hadn't heard

Austin return. Instead, I opened my eyes and saw a champagne glass floating in front of me. I looked up and saw Austin smiling down at me. "Mimosa?"

"Thank you," I said, grabbing the glass from him. "Where did you get this from?"

"Cheers." He held up his glass, clinking it together with mine and we both took a sip. "I picked up a bottle of cheap champagne and some orange juice when I ran into that little store before coming back from getting groceries. Figured that you might like one for breakfast, but hell, now works." He grinned, drinking some more.

We spent the rest of the afternoon drinking mimosas down on the dock and talking about the past, then moving onto our adult lives. The words flowed easier than they ever had, and I felt more comfortable with him as the afternoon went on. The sun was beginning to set by the time we noticed we had been out there all afternoon. It was as if no time had passed at all between us.

Looking around, we noticed that all the families had disappeared inside their cabins, and we were the only ones left out on the lake. The twinkle lights that had been strung through the trees from other cabin owners suddenly came on, bathing everything in a soft glow.

"Guess we should probably head back and get some dinner," Austin said, sitting forward, resting his forearms on his knees.

I nodded in agreement while my stomach started to grumble. Neither of us had realized how much time had passed. "I think that is a great idea. I'm starving. I haven't had a liquid lunch in a long while either." I giggled, letting out a hiccup as I stood, quickly loosing my balance.

"Easy there," he said, taking the glass from me and holding out his hand for me to take. I slid my and into his and together we made our way through the snow back to the cabin.

8

Austin

We returned to the cabin, and Kristy headed into the bedroom to change, while I turned on the fireplace and got the oven heating. Once she reappeared, I then went into the bedroom and changed as well. Now we stood in the kitchen where Kristy was busy making the Caesar salad, while I pulled the frozen lasagna from the freezer and placed it into the hot oven. Then I grabbed the baguette and began making garlic bread to go along with our meal. I had just spread the butter when Kristy turned to me.

"I don't want you to get angry when I say this." Kristy's voice shook as she spoke, and she took a sip of her water before she continued.

"Okay."

"I really don't understand why Laura, God rest her soul, went after another guy."

I got quiet. I knew the reason all too well, and that reason had been haunting me a lot over the past twenty-four hours. "What do you mean?"

"Well, it's just... you're so awesome. I mean, you made me coffee and breakfast in bed. You taught me how to skip rocks." She let out this cute giggle. "You kept me fed with mimosas all day. I meant it when I said you were the best non-boyfriend boyfriend I've ever had."

I reached for the garlic without saying anything and then stopped when I felt her hand on my shoulder. "Austin."

I closed my eyes and stood there, allowing the memories of Laura to rush through my mind once again. I could remember the arguments, the fighting, the yelling that happened every single time we were in a room together. These were the things that no one knew, the things that happened every single damn day, and it was impossible to stop. It didn't matter what I said or did, they happened.

"You can talk to me, Austin."

I blew out a breath. "Our marriage wasn't like this, Kristy. It was nothing like this. We fought all the time, we never agreed on anything. If I said I wanted lasagna, she suddenly didn't like lasagna. Whenever we were in the kitchen together, we always ended up in a fight instead of knowing exactly what to do without being told. If I went to make the salad, she was going to do it. We fought all the damn time, and that got old really fast. It got so bad that I would prefer to spend my days at work, even when I wasn't working, just so I didn't have to fight with her."

"Well, surely you knew that about her before you married her?"

"I did and I didn't. Sure, we fought, but who doesn't fight. She was the one who wanted to get married. She was convinced we were perfect for one another, and that once we worked everything out, we would be fine. That is until we weren't perfect for one another and we couldn't fix it."

"But if you knew that..."

"I knew it deep down inside I guess. However, on the outside, we made sense. It was almost like it was expected of us really. Her parents, my parents, Addie, you, everyone thought we were the perfect couple, when in fact, they couldn't have been more wrong."

"Can I be honest with you?"

"Better than anyone I know," I said, grabbing my coke and taking a gulp.

Kristy paused long enough that I turned around and looked at her. She had tears in her eyes, and she swallowed hard before she quietly spoke. "I was really hurt that I wasn't invited to the wedding."

I didn't know what to say. That had been another huge fight between Laura and me. I watched as those giant tears slipped out of her eyes and down her cheeks, but she brushed them away as fast as they had fallen and turned her back on me to get back to the salad.

"I know, and I'm sorry about that." I watched as she nodded.

She'd been on the invite list, and it hadn't been my choice not to invite her. She'd been as big a part of my life as my own sister. Laura, however, had cornered me one night after we'd been at my parents' going over the guest list. She was convinced that Kristy had a crush on me and she out and out refused to have her attend the wedding. We'd had a huge fight over it. So big, in fact, that we didn't speak for a couple of days. I had actually thought of calling off the entire wedding over it. It had eaten at me the entire weekend, and I hadn't mentioned anything to anyone except Addie. She told me that Kristy would understand, but I begged her not to say anything and I would just tell her that we couldn't afford to invite any extra people. I had tried to talk to her, but every time I looked into her I eyes, the words had escaped me. So, instead of telling her, I never said a word and just never sent the invitation. Truth was, Laura had been wrong. It wasn't Kristy who had the crush. In hindsight, I was glad she wasn't there because I wasn't sure that I would have gotten married that day had Kristy of been there.

The oven timer rang, interrupting what I was going to say, and I grabbed the oven mitt from the counter and opened the door, the aroma of lasagna filling the room.

"It's done! Is that salad ready?" I asked, changing the subject.

"Yes."

Kristy quickly cleared a space on the counter, putting down a couple of hot plates for me to set the lasagna on, and I removed the lid to let it cool down. She passed me the garlic bread, and I slid it into the oven.

Once she had plated the salad, I cut the lasagna and pulled the perfectly cooked garlic bread from the oven and carried the plates over to the small dinette table. She followed behind me with a bottle of wine and two glasses.

Dinner had been perfect, and after we ate, we cleaned up the area together. "They are having a huge campfire tonight down near the hotel. Did you want to go?" I asked, drying the last plate and putting it back in the cupboard.

"No, I think I just want to stay in tonight. We can make smores over the stove and watch a movie."

I let out a laugh. "We haven't done that since our teens."

"Speak for yourself. I happen to make smores all the time that way," Kristy said, pulling a chocolate bar and bag of marshmallows from the bag on the counter and holding them up.

"Okay, well, one thing I am sure of is that I am not letting you cook the marshmallows. I remember what happened when we were younger, and I shudder to think you do this at home alone." I said, taking the bag from her hand.

"What?" she asked, looking up at me with innocent eyes.

"Really? You have to ask? You almost burned the

kitchen down, remember? The marshmallow caught on fire and you went bananas waving it in the air."

"I was trying to put it out." She shrugged.

I laughed. "I think you might have been the reason I became a firefighter."

Kristy laughed at the memory. "Glad I could help, I guess, but seriously, it was frightening," she said, shrugging.

"That is the exact reason I will take over cooking the marshmallows."

She smiled innocently up at me and shrugged. "All right then, I'm in charge of the crackers and chocolate."

"Perfect, they don't involve fire, so we are good." I said winking at her.

An hour later, both of us showered, we had graham crackers sprawled on the counter, pieces of chocolate on top of one of the crackers, while I stood cooking the marshmallows over the flame on the stove.

"You always cook them so perfectly too," she said, watching in amazement. "I always burn them."

"Not always. I remember the one time that you cooked one perfectly," I said, winking at her. I was just about to say something when the marshmallow caught on fire. I quickly blew it out and looked at her. "See, not perfect all the time," I said, laughing as Kristy smacked me across the abs.

"Fine, that one will be mine." I grinned, placing the gooey cooked marshmallow on top of the cracker.

We took our smores into the living room and sat on the

floor, watching a movie, while we ate them. As she popped the last bite of her smore into her mouth, Kristy looked over at me, grinning. "Those were great!" She giggled, her lower lip covered in chocolate and marshmallow.

"You, ah, have some stuff on your lip," I said, wiping my own lip in jest.

She wiped the same side, which was the opposite side of which the chocolate and marshmallow sat.

"Other side."

This time she missed it completely and continued to laugh, flopping down on the blanket we had layed out.

"Come here," I said, leaning overtop of her.

She looked up at me and her laughing slowly stopped as I wiped the mess of chocolate and marshmallow away with my thumb. The look in her eyes stopped me, and before I could stop myself, I bent and kissed her.

We were both hesitant at first, and after a couple lip grazes, we fell into a rhythm. Without taking my lips from hers, I fumbled with the remote, finally turning the TV off. I wanted silence, I wanted it to be just me and her. I wanted to get lost in her and forget everything. As our kiss deepened, I felt myself growing hard, and I hoped she couldn't feel me. I didn't want her to think that was all I wanted. The memory fell far from my mind the second she wrapped her arms around my neck, her hand resting on my cheek. She ran her fingers through my hair, sending shivers through me.

I had to pull away. It had been so long since I had been

near a woman, I feared I was going to explode. I noticed almost instantly the pout that fell across her face. She had no worries. There was no way in hell that I was done with her. I just needed to collect myself. I scooped her up in my arms and stood and effortlessly carried her into the bedroom.

She wrapped her arms around my neck, kissing my lips as I carried her into the bedroom and kicked the door shut. I placed her gently on the bed and reached behind me, pulling my shirt off over my head. I looked down at her. Her cheeks were flushed as her eyes wandered over my chest and down to the top of my jeans. I flicked the button of my jeans open and kneeled on the bed between her legs and leaned down, meeting her lips again.

9

Kristy

HE HELD me in his arms as he kissed me, his hands roaming over my body. I could feel my excitement building. It had been so long since I had been turned on like this. I wanted him to touch me, to explore me deeper. I wanted him to know exactly how turned on I was.

He pulled away and now stood at the end of the bed. I could see the outline of his large, rigid cock through his jeans. I locked eyes with his as he kneeled on the bed. I gripped the hem of my shirt and hesitated, but then pulled it over my head. I watched his eyes fall from my face to my breasts, and I reached behind my back and unhooked the clasp, instantly feeling the fabric of my bra go lax.

I lay back on the bed and looked up at him before I

closed my eyes. I wanted him to touch me so bad. I wanted to feel his rough, strong hands on my body. I wanted him to want me as badly as I wanted him.

He didn't move right away. I was afraid that perhaps we had gone a little further than we should have, but relief flooded through me when I felt him move closer. His rough fingers brushed my shoulders, slowly sliding the straps of my bra down my arms, sending surges of electricity through my body. I felt my nipples harden when the cold air brushed over them, and I almost bolted off the bed when I opened my eyes in time to watch as he bent down and took one in his mouth. Instantly, my hands went to his head and my fingers gripped his dark hair as he sucked me into his mouth, my back arching off the mattress, pushing myself into his mouth.

He moved to the other before kissing his way up my neck and sucking on the lobe of my ear. My breathing was heavy while the ache between my legs became more intense as he continued, finally meeting my mouth. I raked my fingers across his strong back as he ground himself against me. Instantly, I wished he were between my legs, any pressure to help quell the throbbing ache I felt.

He tore himself away from me and got up off the bed, allowing his jeans to slip from his hips and drop to the floor. My eyes fell down his body and back up to his eyes, then with his eyes firmly planted on mine, he pushed the waistband of his boxers off his hips, allowing them to fall to the floor as well. I swallowed hard at the site of him. He was huge everywhere. I barely had any time to think about that fact as he grabbed me by the legs and pulled me down to the end of the bed, his strong hands gripping the waistband of my yoga pants, and he pulled them off me in one swift movement. His eyes were so hungry with need, I could feel it in my core. He stood there, taking every part of me in, like he wanted to devour me but was afraid to touch me. I sat up and ran my hands over his smooth hips, before leaning forward and placing a kiss on his hip. I looked up and met his eyes, I wanted to take him in my mouth so bad, but instead I placed a kiss on the other hip.

The second my lips left his hip, he placed his hand under my chin and gently lifted my head so I was looking at him. He brushed the strand of hair that had fallen into my face and leaned over and softly kissed me, barely brushing my lips with his. He gently pushed me backwards, and I allowed my body to fall back into the mattress and shimmied back up as he knelt between my legs, forcing them apart. My legs rested on each side of his thick, powerful thighs. He leaned forward and held himself over me, kissing me again. I had just gotten lost in his kiss when he pulled away and looked down at me. Our eyes locked, and I could feel the heat building in me as he ran his fingers through my wet center. I couldn't stop the moan from escaping my mouth as his fingers ran over the small bundle of nerves. He took my breath away as he did it again, this time concentrating more on the small bundle of nerves. I closed my eyes, and he surprised me by meeting my lips, muffling the moan that escaped me again when he slid two fingers inside of me.

His lips left mine, and I lay there with my eyes closed. I was afraid to open them, but when I did, I saw him watching me intently. His fingers slid deep inside of me, his thumb concentrating once again on that small bundle of nerves. I ran my hands over his back, running my one hand over his hip to his cock. I could already feel the bead of precum forming as I stroked him once.

"Fuck," he hissed, closing his eyes while I ran my hand over him again.

I wanted to feel him inside of me so bad, and I could feel the anxiety building at the fact that neither of us probably had a condom.

"I want to be inside of you," he breathed into my ear, sliding another finger into me and meeting my lips, kissing me deeply.

The second those words left his lips, I realized just how badly I wanted that too. I searched the deepest parts of my mind, trying to figure out how we were going to do this without a condom. Then I remembered the nightstand and that little basket of goodies.

"Hold on," I whispered. I reached over and grabbed the basket that contained all the stuff I had found earlier. I grabbed the box of condoms and ripped it open, grabbing one and handed him the package. He looked at the package like it was a foreign object, his eyes moving to mine.

"You're sure?" he questioned, studying my face.

I nodded. The silence in the room was almost deafening as he looked from me back to the package. He was hesitant at first, but he took the condom from me and ripped it open and rolled it over himself.

He lowered himself onto me and brushed the hair from my face, his hand cupping my cheek as he kissed me slower this time and reached between us, lining himself with my opening. I felt the pressure as he slid his thick cock into me.

Sex with him was unlike anything I had felt before. He held me in his arms, kissing me the entire time, while he pumped deeply into me. He was the tenderest lover I had ever been with. He took his time, and before I could stop it, I felt myself tightening around him, my body tensing while I called his name, as we came together.

He didn't rush from the bed or immediately roll over and go to sleep like the others I had been with either. Instead, he cleaned himself up, allowing me to do the same. When I crawled back into bed, he surprised my by pulling me into him and holding me in his arms. My head rested on his chest, his fingers running through my hair while he occasionally placed a kiss on my forehead. We lay in silence, watching the fireplace flicker.

Half hour later, Austin lay softly snoring, and I lay there thinking about what had happened between us. I wondered if perhaps this had been a mistake. I had always been afraid of this type of spontaneity. I wondered what he had been thinking, but then I decided that this wasn't really something that I should worry about. What happened had happened—two consenting adults having a good time. There was nothing to be ashamed of because I already knew that after this weekend there could be no more. His sister was my best friend.

I rolled over, closed my eyes, and tried to go to sleep. Instead, I lay there staring into the darkness, the only thought running through my mind was how it felt to be with him. How nice it would be to experience that all over again. The only problem was that I was in no way ready for a relationship. I still had to contend with Tom everyday at work, and until he was out of my life and I was over that hurt, there was no way I could open myself up to someone else.

I wasn't sure that Austin was ready for anything either. At times this weekend, I had caught a far-off look in his eyes, and when he spoke of Laura, I could see there was still love there, even though she was gone.

I blew out the breath I'd been holding and readjusted my pillow.

"Everything okay?" He mumbled.

I closed my eyes. I had thought he had gone to sleep. I didn't want him to think I was already feeling uneasy about what had just transpired. "Yes, of course."

He didn't say anything, and it was that moment that I decided I wasn't going to complicate any of this. I was going to just close my eyes, go to sleep, and know that this weekend was good for mixing things up in my life a little bit. Then I felt the bed move and felt him slip his arm underneath the crook of my neck, his other arm coming around my waist and pulling me back into him. I closed my eyes, the feeling of being against his hard body almost too much for me to bare emotionally. My body betrayed me though, relaxing against him as he brushed my hair back and gently placed a kiss on my bare shoulder, tightening his grip around my waist. I rested my hand on his, and he placed his large hand on top of mine, kissing me again before I closed my eyes and just allowed myself to relax.

Austin

I lay on my back, my arms crossed behind my head, and stared up at the ceiling. I hadn't slept much. Kristy had pretty much fallen asleep within minutes of me holding her in my arms. I glanced over at her. She lay on her stomach, sound asleep. I rolled over onto my side and watched her sleep. I wanted to wake her so badly, but she looked so peaceful. I thought about last night, holding her tightly in my arms, and about her soft touch as her fingers ran over me. I could still hear her moans as she climaxed, and my cock stirred at the thought.

I also realized that Kristy had been the first woman I had been with since Laura had died. She was the first everything—the first one I'd even thought about touching, the first one I'd kissed, and the first one I'd slept with. I never thought that all the firsts would happen all in one night, but everything felt so right. I just hoped it had been as mind blowing for her as it had been for me. At the same time, that thought frightened the shit out of me because it had never been mind blowing with Laura. We had never been that in sync with one another, even at the height of our relationship.

Kristy started to stir and rolled onto her back. I didn't want her to find me watching her—it may freak her out—so I got up, pulled on my grey sweats, and headed to the kitchenette to make us some coffee. While that was brewing, I searched the internet for the Applejack Diner. Once I'd found it, I picked up the phone and ordered breakfast delivery from them.

With breakfast on the way, I filled two mugs with coffee and carried them into the bedroom, setting them both on the nightstand. I knelt on the bed, brushed her hair from her neck, and kissed her shoulder. "Good morning," I whispered.

"Mmmm, morning," she said sleepily as she opened her pretty blue eyes.

"I have fresh coffee here for you, and breakfast is on its way."

She gripped the blankets and sat up, pulling her hair back into a ponytail and bringing it around her neck to rest on her right shoulder. "Thank you," she whispered, taking the mug from me.

I sat down on the edge of the bed beside her, coffee in hand, watching Kristy take her first sip. She was quiet, staring down at her mug.

"Austin, I..." A knock on the door caused Kristy to stop speaking.

"That must be breakfast. Hold that thought," I said, heading to the door.

Armed with a tray I'd found in the kitchenette, I carried it into the bedroom and set it on the bed. "Breakfast is served." I grinned, lifting the cover off the two plates.

Kristy's eyes lit up at the stack of fresh steaming blueberry waffles and bacon. "Austin, this looks amazing."

"I figured you might be hungry," I said, leaning in and kissing her. "I ordered them from the Applejack Diner."

Kristy's eyes lit up and she picked up a waffle and broke a piece off. "These are fantastic."

We dug into the food, and soon the plates were almost empty. Just like last night, we were still in sync, Kristy snagging the last bite of waffles while I snagged the last piece of bacon. I took the tray and set it on the floor and crawled back in the bed.

A smear of maple syrup was on Kristy's lip, and instead of saying anything, I leaned in and kissed her, sucking her bottom lip into my mouth. "You taste like syrup," I said, kissing her again. "Good enough to eat."

I propped up the pillows behind me and had barely relaxed back against them when she got up on her knees and swung her leg over mine, straddling my lap. I could already feel myself getting hard as I gripped her ass. I knew if she lowered herself any more she would feel me. She looked deeply into my eyes and ran her fingers through my hair, bringing her lips to mine to kiss me deep and slow.

I allowed my hands to trail up her T-shirt clad body, my thumbs brushing over her already hardened nipples, a soft moan escaping her. She lowered her body onto me and ground herself against my aching cock.

I gripped her ass, pulling her into me even more, kissing her hard.

"Get a condom," she whispered in my ear as she broke the kiss.

I reached over. I couldn't wait to be inside of her again, and the fact that she wanted me made it all the more intense. I fiddled through the basket, finally finding one. She climbed off of me for a second, and I slipped out of my sweats. She watched, while I slid the condom on. With her cheeks flushed, she bit her bottom lip and then climbed back on my lap.

I gripped her hips and held her while she lowered herself onto me. I could feel her body shudder, and she let out a breath the farther down she went.

"You okay?" I asked, brushing her hair from her face so I could see her expression.

She bit her bottom lip, closed her eyes, and nodded.

I held her in my arms, her head on my shoulder, and

once I felt the shuddering stop, I began to move, gripping her hips, guiding her to match my motion.

I WAS PRETTY sure we had done every position imaginable. I glanced at the clock. We had spent the entire morning and part of the afternoon in bed. We'd finished once, and as soon as Kristy climbed back into bed, we were at one another again, until we were both too exhausted to move.

Sex with her in the light had been more amazing than in the dark. I loved being able to see how her body responded to me, how *she* responded to me, and watching the pleasure on her face as she came. We both lay in bed wrapped in blankets, her wrapped in my arms tracing the lines of my palm with her fingers.

I hadn't been this content or felt this light in a long time. It was such a welcome feeling to me that I didn't want it to end. I wanted to just stay here for as long as we could, together, where the outside world couldn't get to us, but I knew it was inevitable.

"What time is checkout?" I whispered, kissing her neck.

"Three," she answered quietly. "What time is it?"

"Almost two," I said between kisses.

"As much as I don't want to, I guess we should get ready then." She let out a breath and snuggled closer to me. I could feel my cock starting to stir again as she wiggled her ass against me.

"Don't get me started or we will never leave this bed," I whispered, kissing her shoulder.

She wiggled against me again and giggled. "Maybe just once more?" she whimpered.

I turned her head a bit and kissed her, my tongue brushing through her mouth. As much as I wished we could, we would be late if we didn't get up now, and I was pretty sure Addie had mentioned that there were more guests coming today. "Perhaps the shower?" I murmured, kissing her ear.

I walked into the bedroom behind her and wrapped my arms around her towel cladded body. She pulled out of my arms and crossed the room holding the towel against herself. There was something weighing on my mind that I wanted to clear before we made our way home. She glanced over her shoulder at me and smiled. "What's on your mind?"

"Nothing?" I lied.

"Austin, I have known you for years. What's on your mind?"

She was right. There was no hiding anything from her. She probably knew every expression I had. I sat down and cleared my throat. "Before we do anything else, I wanted to talk to you about something."

She nodded. "There is something I wanted to talk to you about as well."

"You go first," I urged, watching as she reached for her T-shirt and quickly threw it over her head, covering her body from me.

She turned around, and I noticed she was almost afraid to look at me. Something serious was weighing on her mind, and I swallowed hard, waiting to hear what she had to say.

"Austin, as much fun as I've had, and as amazing as these last couple days were, you know this can't go on past this weekend, right? I mean, your sister..."

"Kristy, whoa, wait a minute."

"She's my best friend, Austin. What am I supposed to tell her? That, oh, by the way, your brother showed up and we spent the weekend fucking each other's brains out." I could see the panic building in her.

"Kristy, slow down." I stood up and ran my hand through my hair, grabbing my jeans off the chair in the corner and stepping into them. "I really don't think you or I have to tell her anything. It's none of her business anyways."

"Do I need to remind you who your sister is? This is Addie we are talking about, right? A girl who the second you try to keep a secret from will pry deeper than anyone I know to get the answer."

Kristy was right. Addie never really knew her place. Hell,

I already knew that Kristy would never have been here without Addie's permission, so she would already be skeptical that something had gone on between us. I knew the second I got home I would be grilled about the entire weekend, and if she didn't get a satisfactory answer from me, she would be all over Kristy. Throwing my shirt over my head, I ran my fingers through my hair again, thinking of what we should do.

"So we don't tell her. Either of us. We keep it on the quiet side. We keep it just between us."

"How will we do that? What are you going to do, lie to her every time you leave the house? She will be all over you. Hell, she will be all over the pair of us when we get home thinking that something happened between us."

"How about you let me worry about that. I've dealt with Addie my entire life. If I tell her to drop something, she normally does."

"I don't know, Austin." Kristy straightened the covers on the bed and gave me a worried look.

I didn't want to be angry or hurt, but that was exactly how I was beginning to feel in the moment. I didn't want to have this entire weekend wiped away in thirty seconds. I was ready for more. I was ready to move on with my life. I'd spent the last year and half feeling completely dead inside, first at the fact my wife was gone, and then at the fact that my wife had been in bed with some other guy moments before I was called to her accident scene. I was done with that part of my life. There was so much more waiting for me, and I knew it started with this weekend, with Kristy.

I glanced over at her. She was rooting through her bag looking for something. I couldn't let her worry like she was. I walked up behind her and wrapped my arms around her. "Was it not good for you?" I whispered in her ear. Did I sound insecure? Yes. Did I care? No.

She rested her head back against my chest. "My God, Austin, are you serious? It was amazing, mind blowing. In case you didn't notice, I did come three, no, four times just this morning alone."

"Oh, I noticed." I turned her around and held her in my arms. She still wouldn't look at me. Placing my finger under her chin, I lifted her head until she met my eyes. "Then be with me. Just us, no one else," I pleaded quietly. "Let's just see where we can take this. Give us a little time to explore the possibility of there even being an us." I could tell the thoughts were swirling around her in mind as she looked deep into my eyes. "Just between us."

She smiled. "So, I'd be like your little secret?"

I nodded, my hands gripping her waist. "My secret. If we don't work then we agree to go our separate ways. No hard feelings."

"What will we tell Addie?"

"Leave it with me. I will figure out something. I promise it will stay between us for a while."

I swore she was torturing me with all these questions, and then she leaned in and pressed her lips against mine, sending a wave through my body. "Okay," she whispered against my lips.

"Okay?" I looked down into her eyes, a playful stare looking back at me.

"Okay." She smiled up at me.

11

Kristy

The second I'd said yes, Austin picked me up. I wrapped my legs around his waist and we'd had a quick round against the wall, until I was screaming out his name once again. Exhausted and breathless, he placed me on the floor and waited to let go of me until he was sure I had regained my composure.

We took our time packing up and loading our things into our respective vehicles. Then we took a quick walk down to the lake before we made our way home. Despite my worries about Addie and hiding things from her, I was surprised at how everything felt so right with him. I was even more afraid that things may not continue down this path once we returned to our normal lives. Regardless, we walked hand in hand back from the lake. Austin opened my car door for me, waiting for me to climb in.

"Have you got everything?"

I nodded, smiling up at him. "I might have even snagged all the goodies from the basket in the bedroom." I could feel my cheeks heat at what I had just revealed to him.

"I'll follow you home." He chuckled, leaning in and brushing my lips with his. "That might make for some fun times later," he said, raising his eyebrows in jest.

I watched through the rear-view mirror as he climbed into his truck.

I flipped the radio on and found a station that was just starting to play some Christmas music. As I drove, I found that I was soon belting out tunes, but the closer we got to home and to my apartment, the more an uneasy feeling crept into me. My stomach was in knots. I already knew why. It was the same reason as always. It didn't matter how badly I wanted things to work between us, these things never worked for me. Just look at Tom and me, or Jim, or Gabe, or Mack. Seriously, the list could go on, but they had all ended the same way: with me getting extremely hurt and taking months—even years—to recover and trust again. Would Austin do the same? Would Austin become a huge mistake and our friendship be ruined because of this? That thought alone sickened me.

I turned the radio up to try and drown out my thoughts as I went through the movie reel of all my ex-boyfriends and why those relationships never worked. Maybe I shouldn't have said yes. Maybe I shouldn't have built his hopes up, because if I got hurt, he would probably be crushed, and I wasn't sure I could handle having that possibility on my conscience. Plus, Addie would hate me for good, especially if I broke his heart.

It felt like the longest drive back to the city, and I was never so happy to see my apartment building on the corner. I pulled into the parking lot, cut the engine, and climbed out of the car. I figured Austin would just follow me here and head home, but the second I turned around to head to the trunk, I saw his truck pulled in behind me. My stomach was still turning.

Leaving his truck idling, he jumped out and walked over to me. I wondered if I should tell him now that I was having second thoughts or if I should just wait and see if they subsided.

"You're home." He smiled.

"I am. Thank you for following me here. You didn't have to. You're on the other side of town, and I'm sure you are tired."

"I am, but it's all right. You're right off the highway, no big deal. The roads weren't the greatest either, and I wanted to make sure you didn't have any trouble." He smiled as he brushed a strand of hair from my face.

I smiled, looking down at the ground. "I should probably get inside, get my laundry going. Six comes early."

"All right. I'll call you later?"

"Sounds good." I swallowed. Everything felt so awkward between us now, or perhaps it was just me. I didn't know if I should hug him good-bye or kiss him or what. We were going to be a secret. What exactly did that even mean? I didn't know how to handle this, and it was starting to bother me. Perhaps it was the good-byes that were making me feel this way, or maybe it was me overreacting. I just stood there, not knowing what to do, praying he would take the lead.

"Do I get a good-bye hug?" he questioned, holding his arms open.

I stepped into him, and he wrapped his arms tightly around me. The sick feeling I'd been holding onto was gone instantly but returned the second he let me go. I already missed him, and I watched as he climbed up into his truck, waved, and then pulled away, leaving me standing in the parking lot.

I'd had a good cry once I had gotten inside, the sick feeling finally subsiding while I put the first load of laundry into the machine. I quickly jumped into the shower, and once I was all cozy in my sweats, I went to the fridge to find something to eat. A quick rummage through proved pointless, so I placed an order for Thai food from the little restaurant on the corner, Thai Bay. I wrote a quick list of groceries and decided that would be the first thing I did after work tomorrow.

After I ate and had put the leftovers in the fridge, I sat in the living room with a mug of tea debating on whether I should call Addie or not. I wanted to thank her for the cottage but, I was also afraid of the grilling questions I was sure I would receive. Once I decided I wouldn't call, a feeling of guilt crept up. My conscience getting the better part of me, I decided I would call, thank her, and be done with it. I grabbed the phone and was just about to dial when it let out a loud ring.

"Hello," I answered.

"Hey, Kristy! Finally, you're home. How was your weekend?" Addie asked.

"It was good." I couldn't help but fear she would hear everything I was hiding in my voice.

"How did you enjoy the weekend?"

I let out a laugh. "You were right, it was exactly what I needed." I giggled, and Addie laughed, then we both got quiet.

"Did you meet anyone?"

Alarm bells rang in my head at her question. I wasn't a very good liar, and Addie had known me my entire life. She'd come to know when I was telling the truth and when I wasn't.

"Listen, Addie, I have to go. I have to get laundry started and I still need to eat. It's almost eight," I lied. "Plus, the super needs into my apartment to fix a leaking faucet I've been complaining about." I needed to get off the phone with her.

"I thought he was there last week to fix that?"

Shit, she was right. She had been here when he had come in. "Uh, you're right, he was, but now the bathroom sink is leaking as well. I was sure I told you." I bit my bottom lip. She was going to know I was trying to get rid of her. She was going to know I was lying.

"Nope, you didn't. You still didn't answer my question though."

"What question?"

"What is wrong with you? Did you happen to meet anyone?"

"Oh," I laughed into the phone, "nope. I just stayed in the cabin the entire weekend."

"What?"

"You heard me. Listen, Addie, I really must get going. He's going to be here any minute, and I am wrapped in a towel."

"Okay, call me tomorrow!"

The second we said good-bye, I hung up the phone as fast as I could. The guilt started to creep over me. It was almost as if I were afraid she would be able to hear the thoughts in my head over the phone.

It was almost eleven thirty by the time I had folded and put away my last load of laundry and sank into my bed. I flipped the TV on in my bedroom and picked up my book off the nightstand. I needed to relax and calm my mind before I went to sleep. I had just gotten into a chapter when the phone rang.

I debated not answering it, fearing it may be Addie again. I don't want to go through her inquisition, I thought to myself. She was probably calling to see if she could pry some more. Find out if the landlord did in fact arrive to fix the faucet. The phone continued ringing and, finally, I gave in and picked up after the fifth one.

"Hello."

"Hey," Austin's deep voice came over the phone. The instant I heard it, a warm feeling settled over me.

"Hey. I wasn't expecting to hear from you tonight."

"Well, I wasn't going to call, but then I'm pretty sure Addie already called you, and I wanted to make sure you were okay."

"I'm good," I said. I didn't want him to know that I was struggling with this.

"Good, I'm glad. I wanted to see if you'd like to go to dinner with me tomorrow night. It's my last night off before I start back to work."

I fiddled with the tattered bookmark that sat in my lap. It was too soon, and that would be way too public. I swallowed hard, my stomach starting to turn again at the thought of disappointing him.

"That would be nice, but that would be way too public." I felt awful at having to say that, but it was true. We couldn't keep us secret if we were seen out in town together on a date. Word would certainly get back to Addie.

"All right then, what about a movie?"

I looked around my bedroom, wondering what it would be like to have him here. As the idea settled in my mind, the truth became apparent: I was missing him more now than I thought I would. If this were last night, we would be cuddled up together in bed right now. Instead I was here alone.

"I think that would work."

"Okay, so I will see you tomorrow then. I will pick you up about eight?"

"Sounds good."

We said our good-byes and I stuck my nose back in my book. I couldn't concentrate, and soon I found myself lying in bed thinking about the weekend. About Austin. It was going to be a long day tomorrow, and the longer the thought settled into my brain, the more the anticipation built. I couldn't wait to see him.

12

Austin

Iᴛ ᴡᴀs the first time in months that the first thought on my mind when I woke up wasn't how my wife had been dicking around with some other guy the night she'd gotten killed. I was excited for tonight, at the thought of seeing Kristy. I had all day to plan our date tonight, and I was eager to get started.

I walked into the kitchen bright and early and poured myself a cup of coffee. I had just put the pot back down on the warming plate when I heard Addie clear her throat behind me.

"Well, well. How was your weekend?" When I had gotten home, both her and Phil were gone, so I threw my laundry in the machine, and then went down to the station and hung out with a couple of the guys. When I had gotten home, Addie was in bed and the house was in darkness, so I had slipped into bed and called Kristy.

"Good. It was nice to have time to myself."

Addie frowned. "What did you do?"

"I had a couple of drinks and some food in one of the pubs when I arrived. Then I spent Saturday hiking, then sat down by the lake for the afternoon," I said, sipping on my coffee and watching Addie's expression as she packed her lunch for work.

"I see. Did you run into anyone you know?" she questioned.

I smirked when she looked away and ran my hand over my face. I had to keep my composure and hide the smile that was there at the thought of Kristy. "Nope, it was just me, all alone, in the woods." I shrugged.

"Oh, that's odd," she mumbled to herself.

"What's odd?" I asked, pretending I didn't know what she was talking about.

"Nothing, it's nothing. Okay, I've got to run or I will be late. You'll be home when I get here?" She zipped up her lunch bag and threw that over her shoulder along with her purse.

"Nope, going out with some of the guys from work. I probably won't see you for a week or so. I start back tomorrow. I think I may even take my things and stay at the station tonight instead of coming back here."

"That's odd. You don't normally do that."

"I know, but we are going out tonight, so it may just be better to crash there instead, especially if we get drinking."

"Where are you going?"

"Greg wants to head to the next town over to a bar there, so we're going to make it a guys' night."

I could see a skeptical look on Addie's face as she reached for her keys. I never participated in these nights and she knew it.

"Okay, well, be careful!" she yelled behind her as she walked out the back door.

Once I knew Addie had backed out of the driveway and was on her way to work, it made planning everything so much easier. I'd gone to the grocery store and picked up some food for tonight. I grabbed pop, chips, movie-style popcorn, and a couple of bags of candy. It definitely wasn't my normal diet, but I wanted to bring all the comforts of the movie theater over to Kristy's. What girl didn't love a night of junk food?

Once I had my bag of clothes tucked in my truck, I placed all the goodies neatly in a box and left them on the kitchen table. I spent a little time scouring Netflix for a good scary movie. We'd loved watching them as kids. Although, back then I was more about scaring Kristy and Addie senseless. Once I'd chosen a movie, I hopped into the shower.

I came out of my bedroom dressed in sweatpants and a T-shirt; a hoodie hung over my arm. I wanted us to have as relaxing a low-key night as possible—no pressure. I walked into the kitchen to grab the box of food and found Addie sitting reading a magazine. She took one look at me and smiled.

"What are you doing home already?" I asked, glancing at my watch. It was only five. Her shift at the hospital didn't end until nine.

"I wasn't feeling well. We had a shooting victim come into the ER, and for some reason, it just sent me for a loop."

I knew all too well what she meant. The things we both saw daily were enough to drive most people off the deep end.

"Feeling better now?" I asked.

"Yeah. You're going out with the guys dressed like that?" she questioned, eying my clothes and then the box of food on the table. "What do you have in there?"

She went to stand up to look in the box, but I grabbed it before she could. "It's none of your business," I said, holding the box above my head.

"Come on, Austin, let me see," she whined.

I flicked her nose. "See you later, sis. Have a good few days. You know how to reach me if you need me."

"What about your clothes?"

"Bag is already packed and in the truck. See you in a few days," I said, stepping out the back door and pulling it closed, leaving Addie standing there with an annoyed look on her face.

Since I'd been practically kicked out of my house, I

now stood outside of Kristy's door, box of goodies in one hand and two bottles of wine in the other. I couldn't wait to see her.

I'd barely knocked on her door when it was pulled open. She looked amazing dressed in tight jeans, and a black sweater. "Your movie theatre experience is here." I leaned in and kissed her cheek.

"Oh. I thought we were going to the theater," she said, glancing down at herself and then at me. "I'm a little over-dressed," she said, biting her bottom lip and blushing.

"You look perfect! I just figured since you didn't want to do dinner that maybe a public movie theater wasn't a good idea either. So, instead of going out, I brought everything to you. Pizza should be here in about thirty minutes."

"Oh, that sounds wonderful." She opened the door farther so I could step in and locked it behind me. She led me to the living room where I set the box down on the table.

"What are we going to watch?" she asked, coming into the room and placing her hand on my back.

"Well, I skimmed through Netflix this afternoon. Figured perhaps we could watch *Annabelle Comes Home*. We used to watch scary movies all the time, so I thought it might be fun to take a trip down memory lane."

"Okay, but only on the condition that you don't plan on scaring me or jumping out from some random corner," she said, grinning as I began unloading the box I'd packed.

"I swear I'll be on my best behavior. Well, unless you ask otherwise," I said, winking at her.

"Okay, I'm going to get changed. There are bowls and glasses in the kitchen. Help yourself."

While Kristy was getting changed, I opened the chips and popcorn, dumping half a bag of each into two bowls, and then opened the two bags of candy and mixed them into another bowl.

"Wine or soda?" I called out.

"Whatever you are having," she yelled back.

I opened up both a bottle of wine and a bottle of soda and had set everything up on her living room table when she appeared in the doorway. I couldn't help but check her out. She now wore nothing fancy—just black sweats and a purple T-shirt—but she looked so freaking sexy it was unbelievable.

"Couch or floor? The floor we can stretch out."

I glanced at the couch. I knew my height would make it somewhat impossible for me to get comfortable. "Let's go with the floor."

"Sure, just let me grab a couple blankets and a few pillows from the bedroom then." She was back in seconds and laid out a blanket on the floor, then threw down four large fluffy pillows.

A loud knock on the door let us know the pizza had arrived. I went to the door, paid the delivery guy, and brought the hot pizza inside, setting it on the table.

"That smells great," Kristy said as she pulled the blinds,

while I got the movie cued up and pizza on the plates. Soon we were seated side by side on the floor, the pizza was gone, popcorn was now in her lap with chips and candy between us, and the movie was just starting.

Just as the opening credits rolled, she placed her hand on my arm. "This is perfect. Thank you," she whispered, leaning in and placing her head on my shoulder.

"You're welcome. It's better than some impersonal movie theater."

An hour into the movie, we were curled up together on the floor. I lay on my back, while Kristy rested her head on my chest, clinging to me, jumping every once in a while, and hiding her face in my chest at the scary parts.

"When did you become such a chicken?" I questioned, laughing as she covered her face and curled up tighter to me, pulling the blanket she had covered with up a bit more.

"Didn't I tell you how much I hate movies about ghosts? I think you chose this one on purpose!" She giggled, again burying her face at another scary part.

I squeezed her side, making her scream and wiggle even more. "Don't worry, I won't let anything hurt you," I said, laughing.

I was sure Kristy had watched the entire movie either between her fingers or with her face buried in my chest, and even though it was over, she still wouldn't let me go. I glanced at my watch as the credits started to roll. It was almost eleven and I had to be in to work at five.

"Well, I should get going," I said, closing my eyes, holding her close to me. "I have to be at work at five."

She let out a sigh but didn't say anything. I just felt her grip me tighter. I placed my free arm behind my head and looked down at her. In the dim light from the TV, she raised her head and rested her chin on her fist looking up at me.

"What is it?"

"Are you going back home?"

"No, I told Addie I was spending the night at the bar with a couple of the guys from work. I told her I would spend the night at the station. You know, cover all basis," I said, brushing a loose strand of hair from her face.

"Hmmm, I was thinking it's awfully late," she whispered, swallowing hard. "Perhaps you could just stay."

I was quiet for a moment. I wanted nothing more than to stay with her, but I wanted to make sure that was what she really wanted.

"I could, I suppose. Before I say anything though, I want to make sure that you are sure?"

She shook her head yes, then leaned in and softly kissed my lips. Our kiss deepened, and I gripped her ass, pulling her on top of me. I was hard as soon as her body lay against mine, and I ground up into her, my hands gripping her tightly to keep her where she was. She let out a throaty moan as I did it again, and she fumbled for the remote to shut the TV off.

13

Kristy

I woke with a start and rolled over as I felt Austin crawl out of bed, taking with him his warm, strong body. "Go back to sleep. It's too early for you to get up," he whispered, kneeling back on the bed and kissing my bare shoulder. He pulled the blankets up around me and tucked the warm sheets behind my back so I would stay warm.

"What time is it?" I murmured.

"It's a little past four."

"No, I'll get up and get you coffee and breakfast."

I felt the bed beside me dip as I struggled to unwrap myself from the covers, and then I felt his hand on my cheek. I blinked and looked at Austin, who sat there with a small smile on his face. "Go back to sleep. I'll be leaving in about ten minutes," he whispered, brushing the hair off my face.

"Are you sure?" I murmured, lying back down.

"I am. You need your rest. I gave you a workout last night, and you have to be at work in a couple of hours. I'll grab breakfast at work." He leaned over and kissed me deeply.

The memory of last night passed through my mind. I could still feel him planted firmly between my legs. I could still hear him grunt out his orgasm as he pumped hard into me. I leaned up and kissed him again, then sank back into the pillows and shut my eyes.

I'd fallen back into a deep sleep, and he had slipped out of the apartment without my knowing, and when I woke, I took a few minutes while my coffee brewed to clean up after last night. I smiled to myself as I dumped the popcorn that was leftover back into the bag, sealing it up tight. Then I poured a mug of coffee and glanced at the clock. I was going to be late if I didn't get started.

I walked on air as I walked through the office, greeting everyone as I passed by. I ignored the murmurs as I headed toward my office. Murmurs of, "Kristy is in a good mood," "She must have gotten laid this weekend," "Wait until Tom finds out." I'd ignored most of them, except the last one. The last one stung.

I had shut the door to my office and hung up my purse and coat on the back of the door when Jen entered.

"There you are. Tom just called an emergency meeting. We have to be in the boardroom in thirty minutes."

"Okay," I said, smiling.

"Are you feeling okay?" Jen asked as I sat down behind my desk and turned on my computer.

"Yes. Why wouldn't I be?"

"Emergency meeting? You didn't appear to be very happy on Friday."

I shrugged. "I had a good weekend, and I am not going to let him or some meeting ruin my mood."

Jen pulled out the chair across from me and sat down. "All right spill it. Who's the guy?" she asked, resting her chin on her hands.

"What guy are we talking about?" a familiar voice asked, and I looked up to see Tom standing inside my office.

"Kristy must have had a date this weekend."

"Did you?" Tom questioned, a flash of jealousy running across his face.

This was the last conversation I wanted to be having right now, especially with Tom. I glanced up in his direction. "Morning, Tom, and that is none of your business," I murmured.

He looked at me, the smile he had worn now erased and replaced with a look of pure jealousy. "Ladies, be in the boardroom in ten minutes please." He paused, looked at me as he tapped two fingers on the doorframe as if he was going to say something. I bit my tongue, waiting for him to either ask or leave, and was pleasantly surprised when he left my office and continued down the hall.

"You can't say things like that around him," I bit out.

"I'm sorry. I should have known better." She sat there looking at me, an apology written across her face.

"It's okay. He just needs to remember he lost his chance with me when he buried his face between May's legs. Besides, I really don't need any trouble from him right now. I know he's been trying to get me back," I said, glancing at the clock on my monitor. "We'd better get going."

We both wandered into the boardroom and took our usual spots. Tom was last to walk in, and instead of coming in and starting right away, he waited until everyone had stopped speaking and had noticed he was standing there.

"Good morning, everyone. I hope you all had a pleasant weekend," he said, glancing at me.

I rolled my eyes and looked at Jen, who returned my look and once again mouthed, "I'm sorry."

"I came in this morning to some news. It appears that the magazine has been bought out and we are going to be going through a restructuring process."

I barely paid attention as Tom went on and on. There was no way this was going to affect me. I was a graphic designer, for goodness' sake. Surely, the magazine would still need me. While Tom went on and on, I went to my happy place, to thoughts of Austin, thoughts of last night, and thoughts of the earth-shattering orgasm he had given me.

I was still lost in my own thoughts, and I barely even noticed when people started getting up and leaving the boardroom. Jen nudged my arm, pulling my attention back to the room. We both got up and made our way to the door when Tom asked to speak with me for a moment.

"Go on. I will be right behind you," I whispered to Jen.

He waited until the room was empty, and then Tom closed the door. "Have a seat."

"I'm good, thanks."

He turned and looked at me. He hated being defied, and the look in his eyes all but said it. "All right, have it your way," he said, taking a seat in his usual spot. I've been thinking a lot about you as of late. I miss you, Kristy. I want another chance with you."

I couldn't help but roll my eyes. I couldn't believe him. "Are you for real right now?" I questioned, crossing my arms over my chest.

"Yes, I'm man enough to say that I made a mistake, Kristy. I realize that now, and I want a second chance."

"You should have thought about that before you put your face between her legs, Tom. Is it not working out with what's her name?"

He didn't say anything, only looked at me.

"I knew it was a mistake not reporting you when I had the chance," I mumbled under my breath.

"Kristy, please, don't make me beg you for another chance."

"I knew it. So, she breaks up with you and you come crawling back to me. This is just fantastic. I'm done with this conversation, Tom, and I am done with you." I walked over to the door and put my hand on the knob.

"Kristy?"

"What?" I gritted.

"Are you seeing someone?"

I stopped and turned around. I looked at Tom, at the sad, pathetic being he truly was, and then thought to Austin. "Yes, I am, so leave me the hell alone."

I ripped the door open, slamming it shut behind me as I walked down the hall to my office.

IT HAD BEEN A LONG DAY, and I was never so happy to get home, showered, and changed into my sweats. The snow fell outside, and I found the apartment a little on the cold side, so I raised the temperature on the thermostat before I walked into the living room. Seeing some of the remains from last night still present brought a small smile to my face, especially after the whole Tom thing. I picked the blanket up off the floor and folded it, placing it on the back of the couch.

I sighed. I couldn't allow my mind to go there again. I sat down and rubbed my temples, trying to help the headache that had plagued me all afternoon, to go away. I had sent Austin a text earlier, after the horrendous meeting with Tom, but I still hadn't heard back from him. I knew Austin was working, but a large part of me wished he could be here. I needed him.

Once my headache had begun to subside, I rooted

through the kitchen cupboards looking for something easy and quick to eat when I spotted a package of ramen. I'd pulled it down and put a pot of water on to boil. I'd just cracked open and poured a glass of wine when I heard a tapping on the window in the living room.

I frowned and walked around the corner from the kitchen my eyes nearly popping out of my head at what I saw. I ran over to the window, fighting with the lock to open it.

"Austin, what are you doing?" I asked, looking out the window, laughing. Austin was dressed in his uniform and was standing in the bucket that hung from the end of the ladder. The guys down below waved up at me as I looked down. "Is this your idea of keeping this a secret?"

He chuckled and ran his hand through his hair. "I wanted to surprise you. Are you surprised?"

"Yes, but..." I looked down again at the group of guys who all started waving and yelling up at me. I waved back and then looked back to Austin.

"What are you doing?" he questioned.

"What do you mean? I'm getting dinner ready."

"What are we having?"

I looked at him as if he were crazy. "*We* are having nothing. I'm having Ramen."

"Kristy, ramen, really? Let me come in. Let me cook for you."

"You're working."

"Yeah, so? I also have my truck down in the parking lot.

I can run back to the station if needed. I am also creating quite a scene out here as well," he said, looking down at the crowd that was starting to gather below. "You really should let me in before the press shows up. We don't want this all over the news," he said, pulling a bouquet of flowers from inside the bucket.

I just about started crying as he handed me the bouquet of carnations and a little purple plastic bag.

"Seriously, they are on their way. What do you say?"

I couldn't help but laugh. "All right, come on up." I grinned, leaning out the window to kiss him first before the guys lowered the bucket back to the ground.

"Okay, oh, and don't open that bag until after I'm gone tonight," he said, winking as he disappeared from my window.

"I STILL CAN'T BELIEVE you showed up outside my window." I laughed and then took a sip of wine. "Aren't you afraid of getting into trouble for that?"

"Trouble? My buddy is our chief. It was his idea," Austin said, laughing as he shoved the last piece of his steak in his mouth.

He had not only surprised me at the window with flowers, but he'd already gone and bought all the groceries for a steak dinner. He'd come in and cooked up a storm, insisting he wanted no help, while I sat at the kitchen table drinking wine and keeping him company. It was the sweetest thing anyone had ever done for me. He listened intently about what had happened with Tom, making no comment.

I took another sip of wine and stood to clear the plates.

"Did you enjoy that?"

"It was amazing, thank you."

"So better than ramen?"

I started to laugh and set both our plates on the counter and opened the dishwasher. "Much better than ramen. Have you tasted ramen?" I giggled. "Are you sure you don't want any wine?" I asked, holding out the bottle before I poured the last glass.

"Sadly, I can't." He glanced at his watch. "I have to get back to the station soon."

I tried but couldn't hide the disappointment that fell across my face. I knew he had seen it. I turned and poured the remainder of the wine into my glass and placed the bottle on the counter. I was just about to turn around and start loading the dishwasher when I felt Austin wrap his arms around me, pulling me into him. I closed my eyes. I loved feeling him against me. He pulled my hair back off the side of my neck and placed a kiss there.

"Why do you have to go already?" I whined. After everything that had happened with Tom today, I really just needed Austin to be here with me.

"Are you saying you wish I could stay?" he questioned, kissing my neck again.

"Perhaps."

He pulled me tighter against him, this time kissing my lips. "I wish I could stay too, love, but I have to go."

I turned around, and he pulled me into his arms, hugging me. We stood like that for a few minutes before he kissed me one more time. I walked him to the door, kissing him good-bye. I stood in the hall watching him until he was in the elevator and on his way down to his truck.

As soon as I was back inside and had the door locked, I looked around the apartment. I had been alone for a year and a half and had never realized just how empty my apartment—or my life—felt, until now. Five minutes ago, this place was filled with conversation and laughter, and now nothing. Maybe I was ready for something a little more.

I cleaned up everything from dinner, wiping the counters and table down and putting everything into the dishwasher. Then I shut the lights off and retired to my bedroom. I took a nice hot, long shower, then crawled into bed and pulled the covers over me. The only thought on my mind right now was Austin and how I wished he was here holding me while I fell asleep.

Austin

"Hey, Austin," Cindy greeted me as I walked into the station and by the watch desk.

"Hey, Cindy." I was just about to ask her where the guys were when raucous laughter came from the direction of the day room. "I take it the guys are in there."

"Yep. Tell them to keep it down." She giggled from behind the desk.

I made my way into the day room and saw all the guys sitting around the table playing poker. I tried to enter without drawing attention to myself, but Scott, our chief, and Greg had already seen me.

"All right, so what the hell was that all about there, Reeves?" Greg yelled, tipping back on his chair and looking in my direction.

"What?" I asked, trying my best to play dumb, even though I knew damn well what they were asking.

"You know, the truck, the ladder, the bucket, the sixth floor?" Sean, one of Hope Valley Fire Department's newest hires, asked.

I shrugged. "Every girl deserves a Romeo and Juliet moment."

"Oh, please," Greg said, laughing as he pretended to gag.

The guys broke out in laughter. I just shook my head. I knew their teasing and laughter would be coming when they had dropped me off.

"So, where did you meet this girl?" Scott asked, getting up and grabbing another water. "We are curious."

The other guys broke out in laughter as they all sat and looked at me. I wasn't sure I was ready to tell them yet, but since they had so graciously agreed to be a part of my plan, I really didn't have a choice. I owed it to them to tell them. They were, after all, my brothers. I too grabbed a water from the fridge and pulled out the empty chair around the table and sat down with them.

"I've known her for a long time. Since we were kids. She is actually Addie's best friend."

"Oh, you didn't. You're going after little sister's best friend?" Both Scott and Greg looked at me with a knowing smile. They both had married their younger sister's best friends.

"So, are you guys exclusive now?" Scott questioned.

"No. We are keeping it quiet for now. Just between us."

"Why?" Scott asked, reaching into the bowl of snack mix on the table.

I shrugged. "My sister can be… somewhat intrusive. We decided that we wanted to see where we could take this without pressure from anyone else. Plus, she is my first since..."

I hung my head. Every one of the guys who sat around this table knew what had transpired between Laura and me, and even though I was completely over it, it was still hard for me. I almost felt bad because I was so attracted to Kristy. More so than I ever had been with Laura. I had felt on numerous occasions that marrying her had been a huge mistake, and I had shared that with both Greg and Scott when we started having problems. It just so happened that the problems we were having had been much larger than I had realized.

"So how long have you been seeing her?" Scott asked.

"Just since this past weekend. Not long at all. I just wanted to surprise her tonight, that's all. She had a bad day at work. Thought she deserved a little lifting up."

"That's exactly what I told you, Scott," Jeff said, fist bumping his arm.

"Yeah, okay, so you were right, so what?" Scott said, glancing at me.

"Right about what?" I questioned.

"Jeff bet that you hooked up with her this past weekend. We all wondered why you seemed so happy."

"What is that supposed to mean?" I asked.

"I don't think in all the years with Laura you were ever this happy," Scott said.

Scott was my best friend. If there was anyone I could take the truth from, it was him. He was right. I was happier — on many levels. I had never been this happy with Laura, and she was the one I had chosen to spend the rest of my life with.

The guys all went silent for a moment, waiting for me to say something, I was sure. I felt my phone vibrate in my pocket and glanced at my watch. It was getting late. I was tired and needed to get some rest. I stood up and stretched and looked at all my brothers.

"I am happier, and now this happy guy is going to turn in for the night."

"We're happy for you, Austin. Just take it slow," Greg said. "Now, Sean, deal those fucking cards. I have to win my damn money back."

The guys all laughed as I headed to my bunk. I changed into my boxers and crawled under the covers, checking the message on my phone. It was from Kristy sent only a few minutes ago. I would have thought she would have been asleep by now.

I read the words she had sent. "Hope you made it back to the firehouse safely."

I smiled to myself and dialed her number. The phone only rang twice before she picked it up. "Hey."

The fact that she already knew it was me filled me with

a warm feeling.

"Just thought I would call and say good night." I kept my voice low so the guys couldn't hear.

"I'm glad you did. Good night then."

We both went quiet, and I could hear her breathing softly on the other end of the phone. I closed my eyes. How I wanted to hold her to me.

"Austin?"

"Yeah?"

"Thank you for tonight. It was the best part of my day."

I could practically hear her smiling through the phone.

"You are welcome."

I wanted to tell her how I felt, but I was afraid that admitting any type of feelings this soon would push her away. I didn't want to jeopardize what we had going here. Plus, I didn't want to get carried away with myself. I, too, needed to give it time to make sure I was feeling what I thought I was. I also needed to guard my heart just a little bit. If she didn't feel the same way, it would crush me.

"What are you doing?" she asked.

"Just laying in bed."

"Are you alone?" she questioned.

"I am."

"I opened up that bag after you left."

I felt a wave of excitement run through me at the thought of her opening the bag and finding the item inside. I wondered if she blushed in embarrassment or excitement when she'd seen the vibrator inside. "What do you think?" I asked, swallowing hard, reaching down and palming my cock and squeezing, trying to calm it.

"I'm a little confused as to why you got it for me?" Her voice shook as she spoke.

"Well, I figured when I can't be there, perhaps we could have a little fun over the phone," I said quietly.

I could almost hear her blush over the phone. "Oh."

"You ever do that before?" I questioned.

"Goodness, no."

"Do you have it near you?"

"Yes." My cock jumped as I heard the gentle hum of the vibrator. Kristy must have turned it on and brought it up to the phone so I could hear it.

"Do you want to try it?" I prayed she answered yes, because I was about ready to explode at the idea of her lying there with that toy in her hand, never mind her using it while I listened.

She didn't answer me. Instead, the first thing I heard in response to my question was a slight moan in my ear, and I knew instantly she'd already placed it between her legs. I wrapped my hand around my cock, gently squeezing as Kristy let out another moan.

I was just about to ask Kristy to tell me exactly what she was doing when laughter erupted from the day room.

"Kristy, I'm sorry, but I got to go," I murmured. I didn't need the guys walking in to find me with my hand on my cock, while I lay here and listened to her get off.

"What?" she asked breathlessly.

"The guys are coming in. I have to go."

Just then the door to the bunkhouse opened and the guys poured in, laughing at something Scott said.

"Man I wish you could be here right now," she whispered.

"Me too."

"Well, good night then," she whispered.

"Get some rest. I will talk with you tomorrow."

"You too."

For the first time, I was actually annoyed at the fact that I had to stay here for the night. I pulled the heavy blanket up over me and rolled onto my back, placing my hands behind my head, and stared up at the ceiling. The guys continued their loud laughter, and soon everyone was in their bunks and the place was dark and quiet.

It was going to be a long few days without her, but I had a good feeling about us. I just didn't want anything or anyone at all to take this opportunity from us.

15

Kristy

THE WEEK PASSED RATHER QUICKLY, and before I knew it, it was Friday. I had never been so happy to see a Friday as I was today. I was excited to see Austin tonight. Four days had felt like forever, even though he had managed to call me at least once every day.

He had called me bright and early this morning when he had left the firehouse to head home to bed. He claimed he needed help staying awake, and I had never been happier to enjoy my breakfast while he made me laugh. He was coming over tonight for dinner and a movie, and I couldn't wait.

I glanced up at the clock. It was almost four. Only an hour left, and I could get out of here. I looked at the screen in front of me. I was trying to decide if I liked the outcome of what I had been working on or if I should just scrap it and start over, when my phone rang.

I glanced at the call display and saw Addie's cell number. I blew out a breath. This was the fifth time she had called me today. I'd been avoiding her calls all week, and I bit my lip, debating on answering it. If I didn't answer soon, she was going to know I was avoiding her. I could only play the "I'm busy" card for so long. I hated keeping secrets from her. She was my best friend.

I swallowed hard and picked up the phone. "Kristy Douglas," I answered in my most professional tone, praying that Addie forgot I had call display in my office.

"Kristy Douglas," she mimicked, giggling. "So formal when you already know it's your best friend calling."

"Oh, hey, sorry. I was working on something and didn't even look at the display. I'm trying to get this piece wrapped up and sent upstairs before the end of day."

"Tom breathing down your neck again?"

"What?"

"You know, your ex, the boss you hate, is he breathing down your neck again?"

"When doesn't he? He actually cornered me on Monday and admitted he made a mistake and wants me back," I said, rolling my eyes with annoyance. "Other than that, he has left me alone, but I'm on a deadline, if that is what you mean. So yes, he is breathing down my neck."

"Perhaps you should have Austin show up at your

office, you know, just when he normally makes his rounds. He could always scare him off for awhile."

I almost choked on the mouthful of coffee I had just taken. "What do you mean?"

"He could pretend to be your boyfriend. You know, scare Tom off a bit."

I let out a nervous laugh. "I don't think that would work. Besides, I wouldn't bother Austin for that."

"Suit yourself. I know he'd take care of him for you if he is truly bugging you. Anyways, are we still on for tonight?"

I closed my eyes tight at the mention of tonight. In all the excitement of finally getting to see Austin tonight, I had forgotten that Addie had gotten us tickets to some poetry reading downtown. The ticket had only been staring me in the face everyday for the past six months whenever I opened my fridge, so I didn't exactly know how it was that I forgot. We'd been planning this for months.

I hesitated. "Um..."

"Come on, Kristy, really. You forgot? What is going on with you lately?"

"What do you mean?" I asked, trying to hide everything that I wanted to tell her.

"You are never around. I've called you almost six times today alone, never mind the dozen calls from the rest of the week, and each time it goes to your voice mail. I thought you might be sick, so I even went over to your apartment. Then I got worried because your neighbor, Mrs. Clark, said she saw a firetruck outside of your apartment building last night. She told me it looked like they had the bucket up to your floor, right around your window. I was so scared I even called Austin yesterday to ask if there had been any calls to your building."

"You called Austin?" I could hear the alarm in my voice, which I really needed to tone down.

"Of course. I was worried, but he said it was quiet as a mouse all week."

I blew out a breath at her answer. I was afraid if she cornered him he might let it slip.

"I've just been busy with work. The company is in the middle of a restructure. I know my job is safe, but it's been so chaotic. I've actually been bringing work home with me all week," I lied. "And Mrs. Clark is eighty-seven years old. She can barely see and has the onset of dementia. Why do you think I do her grocery shopping?" That part wasn't a lie. I had been helping Mrs. Clark for months now, and Addie knew it.

"True." She started to laugh. "So, you really can't go tonight?"

"Not really. Can you take Phil?"

"He really didn't want to go when I suggested it the first time. That's why I decided to use it as an excuse for a girl's night. Perhaps I could ask him again because I really don't want those tickets to go to waste."

My cell phone vibrated on my desk, and I glanced

down to see a message from Austin waiting for me. I smiled to myself thinking about our plans tonight.

"I'll text him now and see what he says," Addie said, sounding defeated and pulling my attention from my phone.

"Sorry, Addie. Really I am."

"It's okay. I'll forgive you. Can I pop by to get the ticket later?"

"Yep. What time?"

"I dunno. I'll call you. Let me talk to Phil first, okay."

"Sure thing. I've got to go," I said, looking at the clock that sat on my desk.

"Okay, I will call you in a bit."

I hung up the phone and buried my face in my hands. I hated lying to her. This secret relationship was starting to weigh heavily on me. I blew out a breath and decided it was time to go for the day. I gathered my purse and coat, shut my computer off, and ran off towards the elevator.

I'd only been home for twenty minutes when the buzzer sounded for the front door of my building. I was giddy with excitement when I heard Austin's voice, and I ran to unlock the door. A few minutes later, grocery bags on the floor, he had me pressed against the wall with his lips on mine. I could feel his hard ridge between us and put my hands on his chest to stop him before things went too far.

"We better stop and save that for later," I said shyly, running my hands over his hard cock.

"You are such a tease." He pouted for a minute, then

smiled and adjusted himself. He picked the bags up off the floor and went right to work preparing the food for the stir-fry he was planning on making us. I turned on some soft music and returned to the kitchen opening a cold bottle of wine, pouring two glasses.

"Can you please get me a bowl from the cupboard?" Austin asked, since his hands were covered in raw chicken.

"Of course." I reached for a bowl and heard my phone go off.

"You need to get that?"

"No, I'm sure it's nothing important," I said, reaching for my phone and turning it off.

Once the food was in the pan frying and the rice was on the stove cooking, Austin hoisted me up on the counter and stood between my legs. He placed his hands on my hips and leaned in for a deep and gentle kiss. Everything about kissing him was perfection. I could feel the throbbing building between my thighs when a knock on the door drew our attention away from one another.

"You expecting someone?" he questioned, kissing my neck.

I shook my head. "It might be my neighbor Mrs. Clark," I said as he stepped to the side while I hoped down off the counter with Austin's help. "She suffers from dementia, so she might be in trouble."

I went to the door and was just about to open it when I decided to glance out the peephole first in case someone left the main door to the building open. Addie stood on the other side waiting impatiently. My eyes bulged, and I ran back to the kitchen.

"Who was it?" Austin questioned as he stirred the chicken and vegetables.

"It's Addie. I totally forgot she was going to stop by. You've got to hide," I whispered.

Addie banged on the door again. "Kristy, open up!" She yelled from the other side. "I know you're home. Your car is parked in its normal spot."

"Go to the bedroom," I whispered and watched as Austin took off down the hall. As soon as I heard the bedroom door shut, I walked to the door and opened it.

"Addie, sorry, I had my headphones on," I lied.

"That's okay. You have that ticket? Phil is waiting downstairs."

"Yep, come on in."

I turned and headed into the kitchen and grabbed the ticket off the fridge where it hung. I turned around to walk back to the door but was surprised to find that Addie had followed me inside and now stood right behind me.

"Cooking with headphones on, Kristy?" Addie said, looking to the stove. "With music playing?"

"I was listening to a podcast," I lied.

"Uh huh," she said, glancing around the kitchen. "And two wine glasses?"

I closed my eyes. I was just about to tell her everything when she looked at me and smiled. "Are you seeing someone? Is he here?"

"You caught me." I shrugged.

"Who is it?" she asked.

"Just a guy from the office. You don't know him."

"Okay then, well, I won't keep you. You could have just told me. I wouldn't have been upset. I will get out of your way then. Have a good night," she said, pulling me in for a hug. "Don't do anything I wouldn't do." As soon as I let her go, she looked down to the floor. I too glanced in the direction she was looking and eyed Austin's shoes lying there. I bit my bottom lip, praying that she didn't recognize them.

"It's funny because he wears the same shoes as Austin. They even look like they might be the same size."

"I'm sure lots of people wear the same shoes as Austin."

"I guess."

An anxious feeling started to build, and I almost froze but played it cool and walked Addie to the door. "Have fun tonight," I said, praying she didn't see her brother's coat from the Hope Valley Fire Department hanging on the hook by the door.

"Will do. I am so happy for you, Kristy."

"Go have fun. I will call you later," I said, closing and locking the door.

I turned around to see Austin standing in the kitchen doorway. I couldn't help but look at him with sad eyes. I hated lying to my best friend. I did my best to perk up and smile. "I bet dinner is probably ready. We should eat," I said, walking past him into the kitchen.

We sat across from one another, our empty plates in front of us as I reached for my wine.

"We really need to talk," I said, swallowing down the last of my wine.

"Okay."

"Austin, this is great and everything, but I am afraid that we are just ignoring the inevitable."

"What are you talking about?"

"Austin, I am the queen of impossible relationships, and I am accustomed to disappointment. It's only going to be a matter of time before you get bored with me or something comes up that we won't be able to fix."

"Kristy…" He ran his hands over his face. "I think your luck is about to change. This is totally possible. *We* are totally possible."

"Really, Austin? I just had to lie to my best friend, right to her face, because we haven't told her yet. She's going to be so angry with us."

"So we tell her. What difference does it make? Just give me a chance, Kristy. I really like you, and to be honest, I have never felt this way about anyone before."

I looked up at him. I could tell he wasn't just saying this. The look in his eyes said it all. He was telling me the truth. He wanted this just as badly as I did.

He stood up from his chair and held out his hand to me. I placed my hand into his, and he pulled me up from where I was sitting and into his arms.

"Another week, that's all I ask. Let me tell her, okay. It

might take some of the pressure off of you, that way if she is pissed, she can take it out on me," he said and leaned in for a kiss.

"Okay. One more week and we come clean." I smiled, leaning in and kissing him back.

"What do you say we clean up and then curl up in bed together, watch a movie, and just relax?"

"That sounds like a perfect way to spend the rest of the night," I whispered, kissing him again.

Austin

I HAD JUST DUMPED the last of the spices into the ground beef and mixed everything together. I flipped the radio on, rolled a ball of meat in my hands, and plopped it down between two plates, pressing down to form the perfect burger patty. I repeated the steps, pressing out another perfect patty when my favorite song came on the radio. I sang out the lyrics as I continued making the burgers.

The back door opened and Addie walked in, dropping her bags just inside the door. She looked tired after her shift at the hospital, and she dropped onto one of the kitchen chairs and looked at me.

"Hey."

"Hey, you're home early," I said, pressing the next patty

in the same fashion and flipping it onto the plate. "Every-thing okay? You look beat."

"Yeah, I was called in early. It was a hell of a day, and I figured I would have the house to myself tonight. I thought you were working. I've completely lost track of my days I guess," she mumbled, removing the elastic from her hair. She ran her fingers through her hair.

"Nope, not working tonight. You're stuck with me," I said, dropping the dirty bowl into the sink and filling it up with hot soapy water. "I'm just about to barbecue some burgers. Did you want any?" I asked, looking over my shoulder at my sister.

"Dude, it's snowing out!" Addie said, reaching for the glass I had left on the table and taking a sip of my water. "There has to be a foot out there!"

"So what?" I shrugged. "I felt like burgers, and they are better barbecued," I said, continuing to sing to my absolute favourite part of the song.

"What the hell has gotten into you?" she asked, laughing at me as I missed every single note of the song. "God you sound awful." She laughed.

"Nothing has gotten into me. Can't I be in a good mood?"

"Does this have anything to do with Kristy?" she questioned.

I was about to pick up the plate of burgers and take them to the barbecue, but, instead, I froze, not really sure what to say. This question felt like some sort of trap to get me to confess to where I had been going the last couple of weeks. I had been married, and this was the exact tactic Laura used to use to get me to confess when she thought I was hiding things. I knew how this worked.

"Just tell me. I'm not mad, but just so you know, I am the one who sent you both up to Serenity Lake. I'm practically to blame, since I set you up. So, spill it because no matter how hard I've tried Kristy sure won't budge."

I looked at Addie who sat there with a smile on her face. I thought for a second. Kristy had said she was feeling awful having to lie to Addie and that she wanted this out in the open. I, too, felt terrible keeping this from my own sister. Even though we had agreed on one more week, I had also promised I would be the one to talk to her. Now, seeing the end in sight of having this secret out in the open, the secret we had been keeping lifted off me like a weight.

"How did you know?"

"I'm not an idiot, Austin. I saw your shoes in the hallway at her apartment last night, and your coat hanging on the hook inside her door. I wasn't going to confront her on it, especially with you hiding in her bedroom," Addie said, laughing.

I laughed to myself and ran my hand over my face. "Listen, Addie, you can't say anything to Kristy. I told her I wanted another week before we said anything. I don't want to blow this with her. I really like her."

"Hey, look, you've got the perfect opportunity to make this work, so I promise I will keep it to myself."

"Good," I mumbled and blew out a breath, "because I think, I might be in love with her."

Addie jumped up off the chair and wrapped her arms around my neck, hugging me. I hugged her back. It felt good to get my feelings out in the open.

"You are something else, Austin. It's taken you all this time when I could have told you that you loved her all along."

I looked at my sister and frowned. "What do you mean?" I questioned.

"Come with me," she said, grabbing my hand and pulling me along behind her like she used to do when she was a little kid.

She pulled me into the living room and then opened the cupboard where we kept the photo albums. She pulled out one I hadn't looked at in years and flipped it open to a page. It was one of our family trips up to Serenity Lake. I looked at the images. Addie, Kristy, and I were on the dock out in the middle of the lake. Kristy and Addie were sunbathing, while I sat behind them both, my focus clearly on Kristy. She flipped the page to another bunch of photos, where again in each of them I was either clearly staring at Kristy or next to her. Then she opened the album of my engagement photos.

"What are you doing with that?" I questioned.

"Just wait and see," Addie said, flipping to one of the pages and pointing at one of the photographs.

In one of the photos Laura stood in the background

posing for the shot. Instead of being enamored with my future bride like I should have been, I was looking off in the distance at Kristy who sat behind Laura with a sad look on her face.

"Seriously, man, it couldn't be more obvious. Did it ever occur to you that this was what the problem was with your marriage?"

"The problem with my marriage was the fact that my wife preferred the company of someone else in the bedroom."

"No, Austin, I'm not talking about that. It doesn't take rocket science to know that you were never happy. You were forced into a situation to marry Laura because together 'you made sense' to everyone but yourselves. You never really loved her. That is why Kristy wasn't invited to the wedding. It wasn't because of money and needing to cap guests like you told her. It also wasn't because Laura didn't want her there. It was because you were in love with Kristy. That was the real reason why she was not there at the wedding. Just admit it."

"No, Addie, it was because we had to cap guests. Laura was throwing a fit about how much we were spending."

"You know that isn't true, because I know that isn't true. I can guarantee that if Kristy had been sitting in the audience, you would have been stuck on what could have been if you had of made a different choice. Perhaps you might not even have gone through with the wedding at all."

I slowly flipped through the album in front of me and

then it hit. I had spent hours upon hours and thousands of dollars in couples therapy, and in one conversation, Addie hit the nail on the head. Suddenly, the embarrassment of the entire situation started to hit, and I wanted to crawl into a hole.

"It's not just photographs, Austin. I have watched you with her over the last year and a half. She was the only one you would talk to after Laura died. She was the one you went outside with the day of the funeral after the guys kicked that douche out. She was the one who held you as you cried. She was the one who also dropped everything to be with you during that time."

"She was being a good friend." I shrugged, still not really sure I wanted to accept the truth.

"Yep, she was. She also told me a long time ago that she wished her ex was more like my brother Austin. She's the one who has compared every single boyfriend she's ever had to you, and that is why none of her relationships work. It's because there is only one guy who she wants, and that is you. Just so you know, she will never admit that because she fears she is doomed in the relationship department."

I blew out a breath at all she had just said, I knew the last part was true because she had confessed that to me last night. I stood flipping through the book, letting everything sink into my mind. Finally, I shut the book and looked to my sister.

"Addie, listen, please. I promised Kristy that after I

talked to you, we would talk to you together. She's struggling with this and needs to sort out a couple of things, so just wait to mention it to her."

Addie looked me in the eye and shook her head. "No, Austin, no more secrets. You need to stop accepting less than you deserve."

"I'm not. I am giving Kristy a chance."

"Austin, you need to live your life out loud. She shouldn't be ashamed to be in a relationship with you. She should be proud. Secret relationships are for cheaters and people who really don't love one another. You need to tell her that I know and then tell the world that you are together."

"All right, fine. Just, before you say anything, give me a chance to talk to her, okay. Let me tell her that you know and that you are okay with it."

"No worries. I'm not gonna say anything, and yes, talk to her, tell her."

"I will."

Kristy

I HAD WORKED MORNING, noon, and night over the last couple of days to make sure that I met my deadline in time. I hadn't ever been so happy to send an email to Tom as I was today.

I glanced at the clock, disappointed to see that it was only two in the afternoon on a Friday. I couldn't wait to be finished today. Austin and I had plans to go to the movies tonight once he was done his shift, and then we were going to return to my apartment and spend time decorating my Christmas tree.

My phone vibrated on my desk, and I smiled to myself, expecting it to be Austin. Instead, Tom's name flashed across the screen. I opened the text to find only three words: my office now.

A funny feeling crept through me. I had sworn to myself that I would never be caught again in Tom's office. Whenever he requested a meeting with me, I had found a way to either just send him what he needed through email or made him come to me.

I picked up my phone and feverishly typed, "What do you need?" and set my phone back down on my desk, opening the next scheduled project I had to work on. I hoped that this didn't have anything to do with what he had proposed the other day.

Seconds later, my phone buzzed again, and I glanced down to see his reply. "I need you to come to my office." I rolled my eyes and blew out a breath.

Since that tactic had backfired, I eventually found myself in the elevator going up to the fifteenth floor to his office. I drummed my fingernails on the railing inside the elevator as it lifted me closer to his floor. I glanced down at my watch. I really wished that it was almost time to end my day.

The elevator bell rang and the doors opened. I was faced with a girl, her face red and tear streaked. I recognized her from the payroll department. She said nothing. Instead, she took one look at me, covered her mouth to stifle a sob, and as I slipped out of the elevator, she slipped in and hit the button going down. I frowned. What the hell was going on?

I walked down the hall to the dreaded desk of his assistant, the one I had found spread eagle on his desk, and announced myself.

She looked up from her computer. "Of course. He is waiting for you," she said and smiled smugly before returning to whatever it was she was working on.

I walked to his office and knocked on the open door. He looked up from his computer and stopped typing. "Kristy, come on in," Tom said, standing and pointing to the chair across from him. "Have a seat."

"I'll stand, thanks," I bit out and stepped inside his office.

"Fine, close the door please."

"It can stay open, thanks," I bit out, glaring into his eyes. He locked eyes with me, debating on challenging me, but I didn't back down. There was no way I was going to be caught in his office with the door closed.

"Fine. Look, as announced, the magazine is going through a restructure. Unfortunately, many of the departments had to be cut or required cuts, and yours is one of them."

I looked at Tom. Surely, he wasn't speaking about me. I mean, I was a senior in my position. "Fine, so who am I losing? Jen, Meg, Alexandra?" I questioned, annoyed that he made me come all the way up here just for this information when he could have easily emailed it to me.

"Pretty much the entire department," Tom said, sitting back down behind his computer.

"Okay, so no big deal. I can handle the work, and then I can rebuild it. It will take time, of course, to find the right individuals."

"No, you're misunderstanding me. Your whole entire department has been cut."

"Tom, there is no way I can do the work of twenty people, so you better come up with something. Go back to the new bosses and explain that I at least need to keep three people."

"You won't have to, because you are included in your department. They will be outsourcing your department."

I felt the room start to spin. He just let the words roll off his lips as if it didn't matter that he had just fired twenty people. He sat there clicking on the keys of his computer, probably sending out a notice to announce to any employees who were left not to contact me for anything moving forward.

"Effective as of when?" I questioned.

"Effective today at five."

I glanced at my watch. In an hour and a half I was jobless. What the hell was I going to do? I had rent to pay, bills to pay, a car to pay for, food to buy. I stood there for a couple of minutes, trying hard to let the words process, and that was when the anger hit. Tom sat there still typing away as if I had already left his office.

I glared at him and then slammed his door shut. He stopped typing and looked up at me. "Does this have something to do with the other day, when I rejected you?" I bit out. "Is that why I am being fired?"

"No, of course not. Why would you think that?"

"Because, Tom, I know you. If I wasn't on the chopping block, I was probably put on it by you after that. Am I right?"

"That isn't it. Now is there anything else I can help you with?" he asked, looking up at me, a smug smile on his face.

"No. I will be cleaning out my office," I bit out.

"Yep, at the end of today, you still have two hours or so worth of work time. Just be aware that your key card won't work tomorrow morning, so make sure you have everything that is of your personal property before exiting the building today. Otherwise, you will have to be escorted up here by security."

"Ha, no, Tom, I won't be waiting until the end of today," I bit out. "I will be cleaning out my office the second I get back down there. As for the rest of my work day, you can shove it."

"Kristy..."

I turned. I had nothing else to say to him, and I began walking back down towards the elevators. I could hear him calling my name and turned to see him step outside of his office door. Ignoring him, I pressed the down button.

♡

I STRUGGLED with the box of my belongings as I took the elevator up to my apartment, almost dropping it twice. Finally, the elevator opened, and I made it into my apartment just in time for the side of the box to rip and the contents to fall to the floor. I swore under my breath and leaned against the wall, fighting back tears. What the hell was I going to do?

I couldn't even call my best friend to let her know what had happened. I needed to talk to her so bad, but because of keeping things from her, I knew in a situation like this, everything would just come pouring out. I hated this entire situation, and with my fists balled up, I punched the wall. The second my hand hit, pain shot up to my shoulder, and the tears that began to fall—. Once the pain subsided, I grabbed an ice pack from the freezer and sat down, wrapping my swollen hand in a towel.

I didn't have time to be upset. I needed to take a look at my finances and then hop onto the local job site to find something before Austin arrived to go to the movies. I left the mess of stuff on the floor inside the door and changed into my favorite pair of ripped jeans and a sweater.

I sat down on the floor and grabbed my laptop, quickly searching through the available jobs in the area. After forty minutes of that, I was beyond frustrated. There was nothing in my field, and unless I was going to flip burgers at the local burger joint, I had nothing.

I rubbed my eyes and opened up my online banking. I had a little over five thousand dollars in my savings account and was only three hundred to the positive in my checking account. I blew out a breath and, once again, the tears started to slip down my cheeks. I still had two paychecks coming, but after that, it would be a matter of six or seven months before everything was gone, and that would only be if I were strict with myself.

I curled up on the couch and cried for almost an hour, then I did my best to clean myself up after the meltdown I'd had in the living room. I had just applied fresh makeup and came walking out into the living room when the phone rang.

"Hello," I answered.

"Hey, Kristy, it's Addie."

"Hey, Addie." I closed my eyes, fighting back more tears.

"Everything okay? You sound down."

I felt so off balance it wasn't funny. My best friend was calling and asking if I was okay because she could tell from the sound of my voice that I wasn't. Hell, she had probably already sensed something was wrong from the other side of the city, that was how in sync we were.

I suddenly started having doubts about everything including my friendship with her. It was practically non-existent since I had been keeping things from her. And Austin? I had no clue where to even go with him.

"Not really. I..."

"It's okay, Kristy. Don't be upset anymore. I already know about you and Austin."

The words sank into my ear, and I felt the anger boil inside of me. He had promised.

"What?" I questioned, frowning.

"Austin told me everything. It's okay. He said you were going to be upset when you told me. I already knew, though. I knew it was his shoes inside your door the other night the second I had seen his coat hanging on the hook. I didn't want to embarrass you, so I just played along with you."

Every alarm bell in my body went off as she continued talking. I barely heard a word she had said. The only thing going through my mind was just what I had been worried about: that Austin couldn't be trusted. He had gone behind my back even when I asked him not to and told her before we had agreed to. Tears filled my eyes and everything blurred in front of me.

Addie continued rambling on, while I stood there wishing I could just punch the wall in front of me again, but then both hands would be aching and swollen. Just like usual, I would lose him, just like the others, because without trust, there was no way I couldn't move forward in a relationship with him.

"So what else is going on with you?" Addie asked.

"I have to go, Addie," I whispered and hung up the phone without even saying good-bye.

Austin was supposed to be here in twenty five minutes, and he was the last person I wanted to see right now. I grabbed a water from the fridge and drank enough to remove the huge lump that sat in my throat. I picked up the phone and punched in his cell number, waiting for him to pick up.

"Reeves," he said into his phone. He must have been getting showered because he never answered the phone like that when it was me.

"Hey, would it be possible to meet me at The Roasted Bean?"

"You don't want to see the movie?"

"No," I answered, biting my trembling lip.

"All right, give me twenty minutes to shower, and I will swing by and pick you up."

"It's okay. I can meet you there."

There was silence on the phone, and I choked back the tears that were about to fall.

"Kristy, is everything okay?" I could hear the unease in his voice, and I knew in that second I was going to crush him.

"Yep. I've got to go get ready. See you then."

I didn't wait for him to hang up. I couldn't because, as I spoke to him, I could already feel my heart breaking. I had no idea how I could have been so stupid. He wasn't ever going to be right for me. We would never have worked out, and I felt foolish to think that we would.

With that thought in my mind, I figured I would have felt better. Instead, my chest ached, and ten minutes later, I found myself in the bathroom with my head in the toilet.

Austin

I HUNG up the phone and toyed with the idea of not show-ering after my workout. Kristy had me worried that some-thing was really wrong, and I wanted to rush to her aid. Then I glanced at the clock and realized I had at least half an hour before I had to meet her. If I left here now, I would be at her apartment before she planned to leave. She sounded so serious on the phone. I knew in my gut that something was wrong. I swallowed the sick feeling I had and decided that if she wanted to meet at The Roasted Bean then that was where I would meet her.

I didn't waist time. I hopped into the shower, and then, with a towel wrapped around my waist, I headed to my locker, and dressed in a pair of jeans and a sweater. I grabbed my cologne and threw on a splash before grabbing my jacket and heading out the station door.

I impatiently drove across the city, hitting every single red light and slow driver there was. I sat at the light around the corner from The Roasted Bean and nervously tapped my thumb on the steering wheel, replaying our conversation in my mind.

A couple of minutes later, I pulled up outside of the little cafe and parked the truck, shutting the engine off. I spotted Kristy's car right away in the full parking lot and glanced to see if she was still sitting in it, but the car was empty. I climbed out of my truck and walked into the full cafe looking for her through the crowd.

Immediately, my eyes fell to a sign just inside the door. *Poetry slam* was written in a fancy script on their events chalk board for tonight. That explained why the place was so full. It also proved why this was probably not a good meeting place for us. Talking would be impossible.

I looked through the crowd and finally spotted Kristy standing off to the side. She stood there, her arms crossed over her chest, but when I saw her face, I knew something was indeed very wrong. It looked as if she had been crying.

I walked over and put my arm around her, kissing the top of head, but she didn't move. She didn't step in to greet me, and she certainly didn't kiss me back.

"Did you want something to drink?" I asked.

"I already ordered for us," she said, swallowing hard

turning her gaze to a crowd of people who were getting louder by the second.

I was about to ask her if she wanted to grab a table when someone from behind the counter called out her name and set two to-go cups up on the counter. I guess that was my hint that she didn't want to stay. She stepped forward, grabbed the cups, and handed me mine.

"It's crowded in here. How about we go for a walk," she suggested.

I looked around. I didn't want to be in this crowded place anyways. I sensed that whatever she wanted to talk to me about was serious, and I wanted to find out what it was.

"Sure, let's go." She ducked under my arm as I pushed the door open.

We crossed the street to the largest park in the city. She walked beside me, her one hand holding her drink, her other shoved into her coat pocket. I held my free hand out expecting her take it, she glanced at my hand, but she shook her head and kept walking.

"Okay," I muttered under my breath. "I'm getting the hint that there is something wrong? So how about you just spill it."

She didn't answer me. Instead, we walked in silence through the park until we came to the first free bench. I didn't say anything. I didn't need to ask again. I had learned over my years of being married not to push. If she wanted to tell me, she would.

I watched her out of the corner of my eye. Something

was weighing heavily on her mind, and I wanted her to lean on me. I wanted to scoop her up in my arms and tell her that, no matter what, everything would be okay. Instead, she just sat there staring off into the park, distancing herself from me even more so than she had already, sipping on her tea.

After a bit, I glanced down at my watch. We had been sitting here for fifteen minutes exactly and she hadn't said a word. I was about to try and strike up some sort of conversation when she cleared her throat and looked down at the ground.

"I lost my job today," she mumbled.

"What? How? Why? Does this have anything to do with what you told me about the other day?" If Tom was somehow behind this because she had turned him down, I'd go and have a little chat with him.

"No, it hasn't got anything to do with the other day. They are downsizing. Apparently, my entire department has been cut and will now be outsourced. I don't know what I am going to do. I have rent, bills, my car to pay for."

"It's all right. No need to panic. We will figure it out," I said, placing my arm behind her on the bench. I wanted to let her know I was going to be by her side through all this. That she could lean on me.

"We will?" she questioned.

"Of course. Trust me. Everything will work out. If need be, perhaps we could find a place together."

She started laughing under her breath. "Trust you. That's a joke."

"Kristy?"

"You heard me."

"What the hell is that supposed to mean?" I said, sitting forward. "When have I ever given you reason to believe you can't trust me?"

"Oh, well, let's see. I was really upset when I got home. I knew you were busy at work, so I didn't call you, but then Addie called. I was about to tell her what happened when she started spouting about how she knew about us and—"

I closed my eyes. "Fucking Addie," I muttered. Addie had told her. My own damn sister had gone behind my back and told Kristy that I confessed after promising me she wouldn't say a fucking word.

"It was supposed to be a secret, Austin. Our secret, remember? No harm. We agreed."

"We also agreed on talking to her."

"Yes, together, in a week, but you took it upon yourself and went behind my back. How do you think that made me feel?"

"No, I told you I would talk to her, to take the pressure off of you. Remember?"

"Yep, I remember. I also remember asking you to wait one more week."

"Kristy, she cornered me in the kitchen the other night and asked me some question regarding you. She caught me off guard. She was the one who set us up."

"Don't blame Addie for this, and don't make things up about her just because you are in shit. You fucked up."

My eyes locked with hers. She was pushing me. "I'm not making it up, Kristy. She sent you up there first, and then me."

Kristy turned her head and looked off in the opposite direction, then I heard her sniffle and looked over at her in time to see her wipe her cheek with the back of her hand.

"You know, Kristy, I'm not ashamed of us."

"You think I'm ashamed of you?"

I thought for a moment before answering. "Yeah. Yes, I do. I want everyone to know that we are together. You've made me so happy, and I don't feel that we should be a secret. A secret that we keep from our friends and family. This is something that we should be celebrating."

Kristy stood up and threw her cup in the nearest garbage and turned to face me, both hands in her pockets.

"Austin, I can't do this anymore, especially right now. This, us, you, you're just a distraction. A distraction that, frankly, I don't need right now. I don't have a clue what I am going to do with my life now. I need to figure all of that out before..."

I stood up from the bench, the ache in my chest too much for me to handle. I studied her face and could see the tears already welling up inside them.

"When I said we would figure this out together, I meant it. I'm in love with you, Kristy. I know you think that it's impossible for someone to love you or impossible for good things to happen to you, but they aren't. They happened. We happened, and I do love you. I love you, everything about you."

Kristy let out a gasp, and the tears that followed broke my heart because I had told her the blatant truth. I had confessed my love to her in a way that I never imagined I would. I imagined lying in bed with her in my arms after we'd made love when I told her how I felt. Not standing in some stupid park freezing and fighting.

"Austin…" She swallowed hard and met my eyes. "I can't do this…"

That was all she said before she took off back in the direction we'd come. I felt her literally slipping through my fingers as I watched her run off through the park. In those seconds, I literally felt my heart break.

I'd stayed sitting on that park bench for close to an hour. The sun had set before I decided to get up and head back to my truck and drive home.

The drive across the city was a long one and I was glad when I pulled into the driveway. The house was dark, and for once, I was thankful that Addie wasn't home. I picked up my phone, calling Greg to let him know I would be back in the morning. I needed time tonight to be alone. I needed to sort everything out. The first thing I planned to do was get my own place. I'd had enough. This had been the last straw. Addie had interfered one too many times.

I rooted through the fridge looking for anything that I could just shove into my face before I crawled into bed, but there was nothing quick. Instead, I slammed the fridge door shut and started down the hall when I heard the floor creak behind me.

"Austin, what are you doing here?" Addie's small voice asked.

"I'm going to bed," I barked.

"I thought you were going to the movies."

"Yep, so did I," I muttered, kicking my door open.

"You're also on the job, so aren't you supposed to be staying at work."

"Jesus, who the hell made you my keeper. I think I know damn well where I should be. Don't worry, Mom, I called Greg to let him know. He approved of my decision if it's all the same to you."

"Is there something wrong, Austin?" she asked, as if she didn't already know.

I turned to face her. She looked up at me with an innocent expression. "As if you don't know."

"No, Austin, I don't."

"Seriously, you told her that you knew we were together."

"So what? I also told her I was the one who set you up."

I laughed under my breath. "Yeah, well, she apparently didn't hear that part."

"Is that why you're home so early, because she got angry? Here, I will call her. She gets a little uptight sometimes. Surely, you remember. It's nothing to get worked up over. Give me a couple of seconds." Addie pulled her phone out of her back pocket and started scrolling for Kristy's contact information.

"Addie, don't bother. It's over. I don't need you to call her."

"Seriously, Austin, I know her better than she knows herself. Just give me five minutes to sort this out. I assure you."

I reached and ripped her phone from her hand. "You also assured me you wouldn't say anything. It doesn't matter, Addie, because there is no more us. She broke it off." I could hear the shake in my voice and cleared my throat to hide it.

"She what?" Addie's eyes bugged out.

"You heard me. She broke it off with me. She doesn't feel she can trust me."

"Please, you are the most trustworthy guy I know. Why else would I set you up with her?"

"Tell that to her. I told you not to mention anything to her. I told you just to stay out of it."

"Austin, I can fix this, really. Just give me a little bit of time."

"Addie, I don't need your help. You have done enough. She isn't going to forgive me. We are over. She meant it. I'm going to bed. Don't bother me. I'll be out of here in a couple of weeks."

"What?"

"I'm moving out. It's time I got my own place again."

"Because of this?"

Addie turned and headed into her bedroom, and I slammed my bedroom door shut behind me. I ripped my shirt off, balled it up, and whipped it across the room. Then I flopped down onto the bed. I lay staring up at the ceiling replaying everything in my mind that had happened. It took a while, but soon I had cooled off enough that I was able to close my eyes and shut off the noise in my mind. I fell into a restless sleep.

Kristy

I GLANCED out my apartment window and watched as the snow fell from the dark-grey sky. It looked cold out, but I had no choice. If I was going to get a tree for Christmas, I had to go today or there would be nothing left. Plus, there was a bad storm on the way.

I turned and looked around at the mess of my apartment. I really needed to clean up this mess and stop moping around every day. It wasn't getting me anywhere. I was the one who had wanted this breakup. I had gotten what I wished for.

I wandered into the kitchen and opened the fridge to see nothing but bare shelves. I apparently needed to get groceries as well. I couldn't eat another bowl of ramen if I tried. My life had literally fallen apart in a short period of time.

I slowly made my way down to my bedroom to shower and dress. I walked by the mirror on my closet door and took a look at my reflection.

I had a smear of something across my T-shirt, some remains of some dinner I suspected. My hair, a knotted mess, was piled on top of my head, held by a clip. What I noticed most of all were the dark circles that lined my eyes. They were very prominent, proving the fact that I had barely slept over the course of the last week.

One hot shower later and I was beginning to feel human again. I stood in the bathroom dabbing foundation under my eyes, trying hard to cover up those dark circles, but it wasn't doing any good. When I grew frustrated, I shoved my compact back into my makeup bag and zipped it closed. I pulled my hair into a ponytail and held it up with a clip. I slipped into my favourite hoodie and most comfortable pair of jeans and made my way back out into the living room where I spent the next hour cleaning.

I pulled the boxes marked Christmas decorations from the closet and then made a spot in the corner of the living room for the tree I planned to get while I was out. Once I was satisfied with it, I shoved my feet into my boots, grabbed my grocery list from the fridge, and headed out the door.

I had just finished getting groceries and had grabbed a hot chocolate from The Roasted Bean before I made my way down the main drag of Hope Valley to the Christmas tree lot. The parking lot across the street was full, so I parked on a side street and walked. It would be a lot for me to carry a tree by myself, and I hoped that they would have someone who could bring it and tie it to my car for me.

I could hear the carolers that were always outside the tree lot singing "Jingle Bells" and I started singing along as I walked. When I rounded the corner, I came face to face with two of the guys from the fire department. They were both wearing Santa hats, collecting money for the toy drive they did every year.

"Fantastic," I mumbled under my breath at the sight of them. I glanced around. Thank goodness it isn't Austin's turn to be here, I thought, so I walked over and dropped a five-dollar bill into the pot. I couldn't afford it, but at least I had a roof over my head and food in the fridge. The money went to a good cause. Most of those kids wouldn't even have a meal if it weren't for the charity. The guys both smiled at me, thanking me for my donation as I entered the tree lot.

I wandered slowly through, looking for the perfect-sized tree to fill my small corner. I put my cup of hot chocolate down on the ground and struggled to lift a heavy tree out of the way to get to a smaller one behind it. As I grabbed the tree and pulled it forward, it shifted my weight. I lost my balance and almost fell over when I felt someone grab the tree from behind me. "It's okay, let it go. I've got it."

I froze at the sound of the voice. It was a voice I certainly wasn't ready to hear again so soon, and a funny feeling crept into my stomach. As the tree was thrown to the side, I turned around and Austin came into view. I swallowed hard. He stood there in his uniform; a Santa hat tilted to the left on his head.

He didn't say much, just stood taking me in. At the sight of him, I had forgotten about my hot chocolate, forgotten about the perfect-shaped tree that stood in front of me. I couldn't take my eyes from him—from those blue eyes, those strong arms that I longed to be held in. I missed him so much, that much I knew. I was afraid he would disappear into thin air if I took my eyes off him.

"How are you?" he asked quietly, studying my eyes.

I knew they hid nothing. He would be able to take one look at me and know that what had gone on between us had just about ruined me. I didn't want him to know so I swallowed hard, picked up my hot chocolate, and tried my best to put a smile on my face.

"I'm okay. You?"

He shrugged. "Okay, I guess. Just here to do my part for the charity."

I nodded, looking at the tree in front of me.

"I just came to get a tree. I think this one should do it," I said, stepping forward and grabbing the trunk, trying hard to lift it with my one free hand.

"Let me," he said, stepping in close and placing his hand on top of mine.

That touch sent shivers down my spine, and I breathed in deeply, smelling the scent of him, one that I had grown to love. He looked down into my eyes, and I watched as his eyes moved to my lips and back to my eyes.

"Thank you," I muttered and stepped back so he could lift the tree. We walked to the front gate and waited in line to pay, neither of us saying anything. Finally, the line had started to disappear, and before I knew it, the girl had rung in the tree.

"That will be twenty-five dollars please," she said, smiling at us.

I went to pull my wallet out of my purse, but Austin stopped me. "I got it," he said, reaching into his pocket and pulling out a bill and handing it to her before I could argue.

"Can I get a couple pieces of rope as well please," he asked.

She smiled at him as she handed the pieces of rope to him. A surge of jealousy ran through me as he smiled back. Then I realized I had no right to get jealous anymore. Austin was single, and that was what I had chosen.

We stepped out of the gate, Austin setting the tree on the other side of the fence. "Give me a second." Without saying anything else, he ran off towards his truck. He was back in seconds and hoisted the tree up onto his shoulder. "Lead the way."

I led him to my car, and he placed it onto the roof, then tied it down, making sure it was secure before he said he was finished.

"Thank you."

"You going to be okay to get it down and inside?"

"I should be okay. I'll take it up the service elevator," I said, glancing at the tree I knew I would have a hard time getting off the roof of my car alone.

"I can pop over tonight and give you a hand if you need."

"You've done enough. I'll be okay," I said, avoiding his eyes. I couldn't look at him again or I was going to crumble.

"All right, well, I should get back. I have to relieve the other guys. It was nice seeing you."

"It was good to see you too," I said, standing there, not sure what I should do.

He turned to walk away, and I almost called out to him when he stopped and turned back to me. "Oh, before I go." He reached his hand into his pocket and produced a little box wrapped in red paper with a ribbon tied to it. "I got you this for Christmas. I want you to still have it." He held out the box in front of me, waiting for me to take it.

An uncomfortable lump formed in my throat as I reached out and took it from him. My eyes stung with tears as I met his eyes. There was no way I could cry in front of him again, and I prayed that I wouldn't betray myself.

As soon as the box was in my hand, Austin leaned in and kissed my cheek, his lips lingering there for a minute.

"Kristy!" Austin pulled away as he heard my name being called. I turned in time to see Tom jutting into traffic and crossing the road toward me, "Finally, I caught up to you. I see you got a tree! I was hoping we could go for a coffee and talk." He said coming over and standing beside me.

I rolled my eyes, Tom was the last person I wanted to see right now. I didn't answer him, instead I turned to look at Austin, praying that somehow, I could change my mind and tell him to drop by afterwards to let Tom know that I wanted nothing to do with him, but when I looked at Austin, his eyes were already trained on the ground.

"Merry Christmas, Kristy. I'll let you go." He said looking to Tom and then back to me. He nodded to Tom and then without another word, he turned around, and headed back for the tree lot, leaving me standing there with Tom at my side.

Austin

WHAT THE HELL was she doing with that ass, I thought to myself as I dumped the last of the donations into the box inside my truck. That had been the only thing on my mind the entire afternoon. I was so glad that the tree lot was closing for the night. I wanted to get this money over to the fire station before I went to meet the real estate agent to look at the house, I was interested in.

I grabbed a coffee and then made my way over to the station. I drove slowly by Kristy's place, my heart beating hard as I checked to see if she got the tree off her car. I silently prayed she hadn't. I wasn't going to allow her to struggle. I figured if it was still there, I would go meet my agent, look at the house, and then go to Kristy's to help her.

Then I wondered how I would act if I got there and she wasn't alone. However, as I drove by, I was flooded with disappointment when I saw the tree was gone and there was no need for me to stop.

I had dropped the money off and headed over to the house I wanted to look at. I'd had my eye on it for a while, and when a price reduction had been set, I booked an appointment for a quick tour. I fell in love with it instantly, and I decided to put an offer in. Once the papers were signed, I headed over to Greg's. I didn't feel like going home to sit around with Addie all night and listen to why I should call Kristy or why I shouldn't move out.

I banged on the front door of Greg's house. A loud crash came from inside, and then I heard Greg's wife shout something and the door was pulled open.

"Austin! How you doing, hon? Come on in," Shelley said, opening the door. "Just fling your coat over the banister," she said as she turned with their youngest on her hip and made her way back to the kitchen.

"Greg! Austin is here," she shouted up the stairs as she walked past.

I followed her into the kitchen and took a seat on one of their barstools. "Here, help yourself to pizza. Beer is in the fridge. Make yourself at home," she said as she stirred a pot full of something that smelled much like her famous chili.

"Greg!" she yelled again.

"Is that chili I smell?" I grinned.

"Yep, it's for you guys' next shift." She smiled at me, still stirring the pot and calling once again for Greg.

"I'm here. Jesus, give a man a break," Greg said, coming into the kitchen, laughing, and kissed his wife on the cheek.

I dug into the pizza box, grabbing a slice and taking a bite. "Thanks for dinner," I said, raising the slice of pizza in their direction.

"Who the hell said you could eat here?" Greg asked, laughing while he, too, grabbed a slice.

"Shelley," I said, grinning at her and making a face at their two-year-old daughter who was attached to her mother's side.

"Come, let's go downstairs," Greg mumbled as he kissed Shelley on the cheek and grabbed two beers from the fridge.

"Don't go getting all messed up tonight, you two. I don't need two others to care for," Shelley called after us.

"Yeah, yeah, yeah, whatever," Greg said, waving his hand at her as he opened the basement door and began to descend. Greg turned the light on and hit power on the TV, a hockey game coming to life in front of us. "What's going on?"

"What do you mean?"

"You look like shit, Reeves," Greg said, snapping the caps off the beers and passing me one of the bottles.

"Jesus, thanks."

"Hey, just stating the obvious. Besides, you didn't mention anything about coming here tonight."

Greg was right. I had been planning on going home and sleeping the night away after I looked at the house. This past set of shifts had been a long stretch for me. Everything that had happened with Kristy had thrown me for a loop, and then seeing her there today reminded me of everything.

"I dunno, just felt like hanging out."

"I see. Doesn't happen to have anything to do with Kristy does it?" Greg said, sitting down on the couch beside me.

"No, why would you think that?"

He shrugged. "I dunno, I saw her at the lot today—with you."

I didn't know what to say. Yes, it had everything to do with her. I cleared my throat. "I guess you could say it has something to do with her."

"Why don't you tell me what happened."

I picked at the label on the bottle, ripping a corner off. "She broke it off with me a couple weeks ago."

"What? Why?"

"Cause I fucked up."

Greg chuckled. "Don't we all?"

"True," I mumbled and turned my attention to the game.

"Women, man, are so messed up," Greg whispered for fear of his wife hearing.

"You're telling me, I walked her to her car and tied the tree down afterwards. Just before I left, her ex – Tom, came over to her, asking her to go for coffee. The guy cheated on her with another woman in their office."

"What did she say to the coffee?"

"I don't know, I left."

"Like I say, women are messed up." Greg said leaning into me, whispering once again.

I chuckled and leaned my head back and focused on the game, trying to clear my mind of thoughts of Kristy. Seconds later, we heard loud voices upstairs, then the door to the basement opened and two of the other guys from the fire department came down carrying trays of pizza and a case of beer.

Kristy

My Christmas tree still stood in the corner of my living room undecorated. It had been a week since I had gotten the tree and seen Austin. After Austin had left, I had a fight with Tom, finally telling him not to come near me again. When I got home with the tree, I had struggled to get it up here, and then I fell right back into the same rut I had been in, moping around the apartment, crying at everything and ignoring the world.

I glanced at the boxes of decorations that still sat right in the way of everything and let out a breath. "I may as well shove everything back into the storage room," I muttered to myself. There was little point in decorating anything now. I glanced over at the sad little tree and then my eyes fell to the gift Austin had given me and began to fill with tears, but I quickly dismissed them.

The phone rang out, and I rolled my eyes. It had rung numerous times over the past week, and each time I had run to the phone praying it was Austin, but every time it was Addie. I was still too angry to talk to her.

I had just finished breakfast, and I sat scrolling through the new job postings, looking for anything that I felt might be a good fit for me. Again, I found nothing that even piqued my curiosity, and I got up from my chair and went to refill my coffee mug, tripping over another box of decorations.

I had just sat back down when my phone rang again. This time it was from an unknown number, and I let out a breath, debating on if I should answer. It could be Mrs. Clark. She had been having some major health issues over the past few weeks, and I promised her when I saw her the other day that I would help her with her laundry this week and anything else she might need.

"Hello."

"Hey, it's me."

I rolled my eyes. "What do you need?" I bit out. Why Addie would think it was okay to call here after what happened was beyond me.

"Listen, the cancer charity needs those graphics that you've been working on. Is there any possible way I could come and grab the jump drive from you today?"

I glanced around my messy apartment and then down at

myself. I had basically lived on the couch for the past three weeks because sleeping in the bedroom had been too painful. Tissues littered practically every surface of my apartment again, and my favourite plant that stood in the corner was nearly dead from being under-watered. I looked down at myself and realized I was still wearing the same pajamas I had put on after I had come home with the tree.

"Does it have to be today?"

"Yes, I work at three, and they need them to get ready for the charity event. We have to get everything to the printer today to have them ready in time."

I glanced around the apartment, trying to come up with another excuse, but I had nothing. "Fine, give me an hour okay."

"No problem. I will see you then."

I hung up the phone and took another look around my disaster of an apartment. I blew out a breath, got up from the chair, and grabbed a bag from under the kitchen sink, running around the apartment picking up all the bunched-up tissues from the floor, tables, and boxes of decorations. I didn't want Addie to think I was really torn up over all this Austin stuff.

I had just finished putting on the last coat of mascara when a knock on the door pulled me from the bathroom. Someone must have left the security door open downstairs, I thought to myself and glanced out the peephole to see Addie standing there.

I blew out a breath. I really didn't want to see her. I

should have offered to drop off the files at the hospital, but I pulled the door open anyways. "Come on in."

Addie was carrying a black bag, which she set on the floor while she toed off her shoes. I glanced at the bag and then cleared my throat. "Give me two second to get the images saved onto a flash drive."

"Take your time. No rush. I figured we could talk."

"About what?" I called over my shoulder.

"Things. You know, catch up," Addie said, sitting down on the couch behind me.

"I don't have a lot to talk about. Plus, I have to do some more job searching."

"Oh, that reminds me, here you go." Addie stood and placed a check down in front of me in the amount of five hundred dollars.

"What is this?"

"It's from the charity. It's for the work you've done."

"Addie, it's a non-profit charity. I agreed to do the work for free. I can't take this. I won't," I said, shoving the check back at her.

"You can and you will. Honestly, I don't know why you don't open up your own business. You have great talent, and I am sure local businesses would love to support you."

I looked down at the check and thought about what she had just said. It was something that I could think about, I guess. Yet I had no clients, and it would take time to build. I would need something to do until I built things up.

"I don't know, Addie."

"I do. I know Austin has mentioned that the annual fireman's calendar could use a lot of work. Perhaps you could work with them. Austin said they fired the last girl they had. The photographs are being done now. You'd be just in time."

"I don't want to talk about your brother, Addie. So if that is what you came over here for, just save it," I bit out.

"No, I won't. Listen to me, I am the one who set you up because I think the two of you are perfect together."

"Please, we are not perfect for one another. How could you even begin to think that when he betrayed my trust? You, of all people, know how important that is to me. You know how hurt I was when Tom did what he did."

"Austin isn't Tom, and he didn't betray your trust. I'm the one who confronted him. I knew it was him here the other night when I stopped by because I saw his jacket hanging on the hook. You think I didn't know, but from the time he returned from the lake, he has been acting weird. I know something happened between the two of you that weekend. I'm not an idiot."

"Addie, I don't want to hear anymore. He isn't perfect for me in the slightest. He is just like the rest of them."

"Dammit, you are so stubborn."

"I'm not! Why would you say that?"

"Dammit, open your eyes. He has crushed on you forever."

I looked over at Addie, not believing a word she was

saying. When I saw the serious look on her face, I began to second guess what she was telling me.

"He has not, Addie."

"He has, and you have crushed on him for the same length of time."

"You only say that because you know that about me, because I told you that. Believe me, he hasn't crushed on me that long. He never showed any interest in me when we were younger. In fact, he treated me worse than he treated you when we were younger. If he liked me so much, he would have invited me to his damn wedding."

She bent over and pulled out what looked like a photo album and set it on the living room table. The she turned to me.

"You didn't get a wedding invite because there was no way he would have been able to look out in the crowd and see your face staring back at him. He has been in love with you since we were teens. He married Laura because they made sense. He himself said those words to me numerous times. There was never true love there. They fell into a routine because that was what was expected of them. He has never been truly happy, Kristy, unless he is looking at you. I have an entire album that you can look through to prove it to yourself."

I sat there staring at her. The images that she was after were long ago saved on the jump drive. I glanced to the album that she flipped through.

"Every time he looks at you, this look comes over his face," she said, flipping through the photos.

I turned and took the jump drive out of my computer and walked over to where Addie stood. I, too, began looking down at the photos she was looking at.

"Look, here we are at your eighteenth birthday. Look at how happy he is here."

"So what? We were all happy in case you don't notice the other five people in the picture smiling."

"Kristy, you can't tell me that you don't look at that and see a different look in his eyes."

"I just can't do this, Addie," I said, taking the album and closing it. "He's a risk I don't think I can handle taking right now."

"Kristy, it's time you get over all the other shit that happened with your other relationships. Tom was a dick who couldn't keep it in his pants. The others were just trial and error, something we all go through. Austin isn't a risk, Kristy. The others were. He has always been yours. He has always been truly, madly, and deeply in love with you. Just open your eyes and look." She said pointing to the photographs in front of her.

She flipped open the album to the day he had gotten engaged. Laura stood in the center of the group, looking freaking gorgeous in his arms. "Look at who he is looking at."

"He's looking at Laura."

"No, he isn't. He is looking at you. You were standing

beside Laura when this image was taken, in case you forgot. You need to open your eyes and take a good long damn look. You need to call him, Kristy. Call him and work things out. If you don't believe it from photos, I have about ten years of video evidence from when we were teens that I can bring over so that you can watch."

I took the album and sat down, flipping through the pages. The more I looked, the more I saw exactly what she was talking about. Every picture of us together there was a look in his eyes, a happiness that I hadn't seen since the other night when he was here for dinner.

"Can I borrow these?" I whispered.

"Yes, of course, as long as you promise me you aren't going to burn them," Addie said, looking down at her watch. "Look, I have to go."

I walked her to the door, saying good-bye. "Call him," she whispered in my ear as she hugged me.

Once Addie had left, I wandered back into the living room and slid down onto the floor. I pulled the albums out that Addie had brought and flipped through each of the books. I pulled the last book out, opening the cover, and was surprised to find an entire album that contained nothing but pictures of Austin and me from vacations when we were younger. I smiled as I silently flipped through the albums.

I glanced to the perfectly wrapped present that Austin had given me the other day. It still sat on the corner of the coffee table where I'd left it. I reached for it. With trembling hands, I began to unwrap the gift. Once the paper had been peeled away, I sat staring at a little black velvet box. I swallowed hard as I opened it, and there inside sat a white gold heart-shaped locket.

Tears flooded my eyes. I had one of these when I had been in my teens, and I had lost it up at Serenity Lake. I remembered the day so vividly. My father had given me that locket. He had just passed away the previous summer, and when I had found out it had slipped off my neck while we had been swimming, I had spent the night in tears. Austin had sat with me the entire night, promising me that he would help me look for it in the morning.

I wiped the tears from my cheeks. How the hell he had remembered that, I didn't know. I opened the little locket and engraved inside were the words "I love you."

Hours later, by the lights of the Christmas tree that was now decorated in the corner, I sat scanning some of my favourite images of us into the computer, compiling them into a book of memories. I knew what I needed to do, and I knew I needed to do it now or risk losing him forever.

22

Austin

It had been amost three weeks since I had heard from Kristy. There were only a couple days until Christmas, and I had debated calling her to make sure she was okay but figured if she had wanted to talk to me she would have called. She had probably shacked up with Tom, I could imagine them all cozied up on the couch. The thought pissed me off so instead of dwelling on something I had no control over, I buried myself in work and packing to move.

It had been a long day at work. We'd spent the morning delivering gifts to the less fortunate families in the area and then spent the rest of the day doing drills at our training center. Carrying one hundred pounds of hose in a seventy-eight-pound suit up twenty flights of stairs was not what I called fun. I called it punishment, and I took that punishment like a man, trying to deal with all that happened over the past few weeks.

"Jesus, Austin, you kicked our asses!" Greg said, dropping down on the floor beside me, huffing and puffing.

I picked up my water bottle and squirted some into my mouth. Then I took another couple of mouthfuls before lying back on the mat.

"Yeah, well, you need to work out more," I murmured, slapping him on his back. "Too many wing nights," I said, laughing.

"Yeah, yeah, watch it, would you." Greg laughed as he took his water bottle and sprayed his face.

We sat there in silence watching the last of the guys come running back down the stairs, dropping the gear onto the ground and collapsing beside us.

"Whose turn to cook tonight?" I questioned.

"Mine. Did you want to do it?" Greg asked.

"Nah, I am gonna take a hot shower and enjoy someone else making dinner for once." I laughed, even though my stomach turned at the threat of food. I barely had an appetite the past couple of weeks, and the more I thought about food, the sicker I felt.

"Well, we should get back. Come on, boys, get up. Let's get the gear loaded up," Scott barked.

We got up and began gathering our training gear and loading it neatly back onto the truck. Once back at the station, we hung everything back up and then headed for the showers. I was one of the last guys out, and I walked across our shower rooms and threw the towel into the hamper. I glanced into the laundry hamper and decided to throw a load of towels into the washer before heading towards the bunk room. It was my way of taking my time, so I could have some time to myself.

I was never so happy to see an empty room, and I dropped down on my bunk, putting my hands behind my head. I'd pushed through all the training today, and now I just wanted to rest.

I could already smell the start of dinner, and my stomach still flopped at the idea, even though, normally, by now I could eat my own arm after a day like today. I prayed that it was a slow night. I wasn't in the mood for needing to be on my game. I was tired, my head hurt, and so did my heart.

"Steak or chicken?" Greg questioned, poking his head around the corner.

"Whatever you decide on is fine. I probably won't eat. Not all that hungry."

"You feeling okay? Did you overdo it today trying to be a show-off?" he questioned.

"I'm fine," I said, rolling onto my side. "Tired I guess."

Greg had seen me at my worst, and I knew he was now looking at me with the same growing concern he had the weeks after Laura had died.

"All right get some rest. I will let you know when we are going to eat, and if you want, you can join us."

"Thanks, man."

"Oh, and when you're ready to talk, I'll be around," he said, tapping his fingers on the doorframe.

I watched as Greg left the room, leaving me in silence. I had no idea how I was going to get out of this funk I was in. Only weeks ago, my life had felt so complete. I had everything I needed, and now, once again, I was alone. Not only had I lost Kristy, but I had pushed my sister away as well.

I heard the roar of laughter followed by some whistles, followed by one of our new hires I barely knew shout out some comment of "Go get him, girl." I heard heels clicking across the floor, and I rolled to the opposite side, reaching for my headphones, and rolled back over in time to see Kristy standing awkwardly inside the bunk room door looking around.

My heart rate increased at the sight of her. I had to blink twice to make sure she was truly standing there.

"Kristy?"

She looked perfect standing there, her cheeks deeply flushed as she smiled in my direction.

"So, this is where you sleep when you are working huh?" she questioned, looking around.

I had totally forgotten she had never been inside the firehouse. I stood. "Yeah, this is it."

"Can I come in?" she questioned, continuing to look around, almost as if she was afraid of what she might see.

"Sure," I said, sitting back down on my bunk, making room for her to sit as well. "It's just me in here."

She carried with her a package wrapped in bright Christmas paper. She set the gift on her lap once she sat down and ran her hands over the blanket on my bunk and then smiled up at me.

"How are you doing?" she asked quietly.

"I've been better." I wasn't about to lie to her. "What about you?"

She shrugged, looking up at me with red-rimmed eyes. "I've had better days," she muttered. Her hand reached up to the locket I now saw hanging around her neck.

"You opened it?"

"I did, and I love it. It reminds me of the one I lost when we were at Serenity Lake when we were kids, like the one my dad gave me."

"I know, I remembered."

Her eyes were rimmed with tears. I thought she was going to start crying any second, but instead, she wiped her eyes and smiled at me. "I came to show you something."

"Okay."

I wasn't going to try to win her back. I was going to let her lead this conversation. She cleared her throat and then placed the package in my lap.

"What is this?" I asked.

"Open it."

I ripped the ribbon off and took the paper off as neatly as I could. I flipped it over, and there on the front of the book was a picture of us from when we were kids. I was holding the garden hose so she could take a drink. I remembered exactly when that picture had been taken. I smiled at the memory and ran my hand over the image. I opened the book and began flipping through the pages—all pictures from when we were younger. Each and every memory I remembered as if it were yesterday.

"You know, Austin, I've always wanted you, but part of me always thought you were a risk. With you being Addie's older brother always scared me because, if we didn't work, I feared I wouldn't have been able to stay friends with her. So, I lived my life and dated all these losers and watched the one man I really wanted, marry someone else. Well, I am done. I have never been one to take risks. That is… until now. I feel that we have been blessed with the option of a second chance."

I couldn't help but stop looking at the images in the book to look at her. Her cheeks were flushed more now than they were when she first arrived.

She reached over and took my hand in hers. "But I realized something. You were never a risk. You are the real deal. You always were."

"What about Tom?"

"Tom?"

"Yeah the day at the tree lot, he came over and wanted to have coffee with you. I thought you guys got back together."

Kristy shook her head, "No Austin, after you left I was very quick at telling him where he could go."

I couldn't help but wrap my arm around her and pull her

into me. She wrapped her arms around my neck and pulled me close to her.

"I've given it some thought. I'm going to open up my own design company. It's going to take a lot of work, but you know what? You taught me not to be afraid to take risks."

I put the book aside and picked her up from where she sat and placed her on my lap. "I swear to you I would never betray your trust."

"I know, Austin. I was upset at many things. It wasn't just the fact that you had told Addie. I think because I feel so close to you and you were there at the time, I decided to take everything out on you. It wasn't right, and I didn't mean what I said. I realized that after I got home, but I couldn't call you. I was too embarrassed. I hurt you, and it killed me inside."

"It's okay, Kristy," I said, brushing the hair from her face. I placed both hands on her cheeks and kissed her. As soon as our lips touched, it was like my entire soul lit on fire. I felt whole again.

As soon as we parted, she looked at me as if there were still an unanswered question between us. "What is it?" I questioned.

"You looked through the book, but I think you may have missed the last page, which is the most important part," she said, picking the book up and opening it to the last page.

I flipped to the last page in the book and read the

words. A wave of emotion came over me at first, and then I looked up at her, a smile coming to my lips. "Yes. The answer is yes. Of course, I'll forgive you." I wrapped my arms around her tighter, pulling her into me and kissing her deeply.

"Take me home," she moaned in my ear as I kissed her neck. The sound of her voice went straight to my cock. I was just about to bust as she ground down on my lap when she met my lips again. "Let's go," I said in between kisses.

At this point, the only thing that would take my attention from making the most beautiful girl in the world mine would be the fire alarm. We got up off my bunk and were just about to the door when the alarm sounded. Kristy stopped in her tracks, and I looked to her.

"You've got to go don't you?"

I knew that disappointment lined my face, and I nodded at her as the guys came running in, opening their lockers and pulling out their gear, while Kristy stood looking at me.

"Let's go, Reeves," Scott called out.

"Come to my place once you are done?" Kristy whispered and ran back to my bunk and took the book she'd made me, while I ran to my locker. She reached into her pocket and pulled out a key then ran over to me and placed it in my hand and closed my fingers around it. "See you tonight?"

"You got it. I will see you in a bit." I kissed her quickly and continued pulling my gear on.

23

Kristy

I sat in the living room watching the end of a Christmas movie. I yawned and glanced at the clock and saw that it was almost eleven. Austin had been on that call for the past seven hours, and I was beginning to get a little worried.

As the anxiety crept through me, I figured it may be best for me to go to bed. I knew Austin would eventually come, so I locked the door and wandered into the bedroom, slipped off my pajama pants, and climbed into bed. I grabbed my book from the nightstand and began reading, hoping that it would keep me awake until Austin arrived.

I woke to what sounded like a thud in the apartment and sat up, listening hard. I glanced at the clock. I was shocked to see it was already one in the morning. I found my book lying next to me and moved it to the nightstand when I heard another noise. I slipped out from under the covers and went to the door, stopping to listen again before I cautiously walked down the hall towards the living room. I could see the entryway light on, and I poked my head around the corner to see Austin, with his back to me, fiddling with the lock on the door.

"What time is it?" I questioned quietly, trying not to scare him.

He turned his head and looked at me. "Hey, it's a little past one. I was trying not to wake you. I can't get this locked," he said, jiggling the lock more.

I was about to step forward to show him how to lock the broken lock when I heard it click shut. He leaned down and pulled off his boots. He was still wearing his uniform, which meant he had probably just left the scene and drove right here. He dropped his heavy coat onto the floor.

I stood there staring at him, watching as his muscles flexed underneath the T-shirt he was wearing. I realized I had jumped out of bed in a hurry to see who was inside, and I was wearing nothing but the T-shirt I had gone to bed in. I realized that he, too, had noticed, and his eyes washed over me and he took a step toward me.

"I'm sorry I took so long," he whispered, stepping closer to me. "You do know that you've been on my mind all night. Where did we leave off?" he growled.

In one swift motion he had swooped me up in his arms,

kissing me as my legs wrapped around his waist, while he carried me down the hall to my bedroom.

He placed me onto the bed, gripped the hem of my shirt, and pulled it off me, the look in his eyes one of hunger, want, and need. He reached behind him and pulled off his shirt, exposing his rock-hard abs to me. I leaned forward and ran my fingers over his rippled muscles. His hand found my chin, and he tilted my head up so he could look into my eyes as he undid his belt buckle, dropping his pants to the floor. I couldn't help but allow my eyes to run over his body. He pushed me back and crawled in between my legs and held himself overtop of me, looking down into my eyes.

"It was a long night, and I'm kind of tired," he whispered.

"That's okay," I said, running my hand down his cheek.

"So, I might not be able to—"

I pressed my finger to his lips, silencing him. "It's okay. We don't have to do anything."

He said nothing, just took hold of my hand and ran it over himself, shuddering at my touch. He was hard as a rock, and I instantly knew that that had not been what he was talking about. "I was going to say I might not be able to do it more than one time." He chuckled.

He lowered himself down and kissed me, moving his lips over my ear, down to my neck, and then my shoulder. He ran his hands up my body, gently cupping my breast, and then allowed his lips to travel to my already hardened nipple.

The sound of my moan echoed through the room as he twirled his tongue around it and sucked me gently into his mouth before letting it go and coming up to meet my mouth again.

"I missed you," he whispered.

"I missed you too," I answered back, opening my legs so he could rest between them.

He leaned on his forearms, staring down into my face, gently brushing my hair back with his fingers. "Do you have any condoms?" he asked, looking down at me tenderly.

I blushed. I wanted to feel him inside of me, not him with a layer of protection between us. I locked eyes with him and shyly shook my head no.

"That's a bit of a problem," he murmured, looking at the clock. "Stores are probably closed. We used all the ones from that weekend away?"

I nodded and brought my lips to his ear. "I don't think we need one," I whispered.

He looked into my eyes. I was sure he could feel my heart thumping with nervousness and excitement as I waited for him to say something.

"Are you sure?" he asked as he studied my eyes.

"I'm sure."

I couldn't tell what he was thinking, and for a minute, I was worried that perhaps I had crossed a line and that this was going to be taking too big of a step. That thought was soon squashed when he brought his lips to mine, sliding his tongue between my lips and through my mouth. It was slowest, deepest, most sensual kiss we had shared since we had been together.

He ran his hands over my body, and then I felt his hand between us as he pumped himself a couple of times before he aligned himself with my opening. He inched in slowly, the deep groan coming from his lips as he continued inching inside of me.

It felt different. We felt closer, and I could feel every part of him inside of me. Once he was fully seated, he held himself there, taking a moment to kiss me again. When we parted, he looked down at me as he pulled himself out and pumped back into me, all the way to the hilt. I couldn't hold back the moan that slipped between my lips.

I tried to open my eyes so I, too, could watch him, watch his expression as he sank himself inside of me, but every time I thought I would be able to, he buried himself so deep inside of me, which felt so good I had no choice but to close my eyes.

We took our time, slow and steady, building us both up, and then he would stop, allowing us both to come back down. It was the most sensual love making I had ever experienced, and when we couldn't fight our orgasms any longer, we both came, quivering and holding onto one another, completely breathless.

Ten minutes later, I lay wrapped in his arms, pressed

against his warm body, with my eyes closed. Everything once again felt complete, and I rolled over so I could bury my face into his chest. I couldn't help the tears that began to fall, my body shaking.

"Hey, what's wrong?" Austin's deep, tired voice asked as he pulled me closer to him.

I sniffled. "I can't believe I almost lost you. That I pushed you away."

He didn't say anything right away. Instead, he kissed my forehead and smoothed my hair. "I'm here now. I'm not going anywhere. Unless, of course, you want me to. Honestly, make-up sex it the best kind. It's probably my favorite." He met my lips, slowly kissing me as he held me closer to him than I even thought possible.

I FELT the bed dip and opened my eyes. The room was still dark, and I looked over my shoulder to see Austin sitting on the edge of the bed. I rolled over and placed my hand on his hip. "What is it?" I murmured.

"It's time to get up. I have to get back to the station."

"Really?" I whined.

"Yep."

I glanced at the clock. It was only five, which meant Austin had had less than three hours worth of sleep. "I'll get up and make you something to eat," I said.

"No, babe, it's early. Go back to sleep. You need your

rest," he said, pulling the covers back up around me and kissing me.

He wanted me to go back to sleep, but as soon as I had heard him climb into the shower, I got up. I headed to the kitchen where I put on some coffee and began making oatmeal and toast. He was under-slept and tired, and I didn't want him leaving here without something in his stomach.

I busied myself, and soon I felt his hands on my hips. "What are you doing?" he whispered, kissing my ear.

"Making you breakfast."

Austin distracted me for a minute, kissing me, and then sat down at the table, while I poured the oatmeal into the bowls.

"I could get used to this." He chuckled. "Addie usually throws me a cold piece of toast and a reheated cup of coffee on my way out the door."

"That sounds exactly like Addie." I laughed. She was all about quick foods that she could eat in two seconds because of her job. I placed the bowl of oatmeal in front of him, along with yogurt and blueberries, and sat down across from him after pouring two cups of coffee.

"This looks great. Really, you didn't have to."

"I'll make you breakfast anytime." I winked.

"I'd love that. So tell me, when are you planning on starting your business?"

"Well, I was thinking the new year. I need a bunch of things first, and it's going to put a significant dent into my savings, but the sooner I get it done, the quicker I can get started."

Austin nodded. "Well, I was thinking this morning in the shower. Would it help you if you had a roommate?"

"Yeah, most definitely, but this is a one-bedroom apartment. I'm not sure I want to turn the living room into a bedroom just so I have someone to share the rent with, if you know what I mean."

"No, I get it. Although I wasn't quite thinking that. I thought maybe you could move in with me."

I looked up from my breakfast and smiled. "Austin, that would be great, and it's really thoughtful, but I don't know if our relationship could stand having Addie in our faces every morning or listening to us every night." I chuckled. "I mean, I love her to death, but..."

Austin held up his hand to stop me. "What if I told you I bought a house and that it would just be us."

"You what?"

"I bought a house. I want you to move in with me." A slow smile spread across his lips as he got up from the table and placed his empty bowls in the sink.

For a minute, I sat there shocked, and then I got up and walked over to him. He turned as I approached, and I threw my arms around his neck. "Yes," I said, standing on my tiptoes to try and reach his lips. "Yes, I will move in with you."

He pulled me into his arms, lifted me up, and kissed me hard.

EPILOGUE

Kristy - Three months later

Moving day came quicker than we both had thought. I had been busy during the beginning of the year getting things up and running for my business and had managed to secure a couple of accounts. Austin had ended up moving in with me right after Christmas, to help me until we took possession of the house.

We'd begun moving some things that we could do ourselves the day prior, but today we had the guys from the station coming to give us a hand. The last load was on the way over from my apartment, and Austin's stuff from Addie's, plus, the storage unit he had was now sitting in the middle of the rooms of the house.

"That's it!" Greg said, coming and dropping the last box from the back of his truck onto the kitchen floor.

"God, you have a lot of stuff," Greg said, staring at the mess of boxes.

"It's not all mine. Austin had the entire storage unit remember." I laughed as the guys flopped down onto the couch that sat in the middle of the living room.

"We remember!" They all let out a laugh.

I grabbed four beers from the fridge, opening each of them and then carrying them into the guys. "Pizza and wings should be here soon," I said, and sat down on the arm of Austin's chair. "I ordered it about forty minutes ago."

"Can't wait. I'm starving." Austin chuckled. "What about you guys?"

"Seriously, you guys are slave drivers. We are starving. We weren't sure if you were going to feed us or not," Greg said, and the guys all started to laugh.

"Feeding everyone but you there, Greg." Austin chuckled, taking a swig of his beer.

I got up, leaving them to their talk, and went into the kitchen and began unpacking dishes and putting them away.

"Help!" I heard from outside and looked out the window to see Addie standing holding three trays of pizza and two large containers of what must have been the wings with no way to be able to open the door.

I laughed seeing her struggle as I opened the back door and took some of the food from her. "Thanks!" I said.

"I ran into the pizza guy in the driveway. You guys have

enough food here to feed an army." She laughed, stepping inside and handing me the other pizza boxes I couldn't take from her in the first place.

"That's because we new you were coming," Austin said, coming into the kitchen to give us a hand.

"Haha....very funny," Addie said, rolling her eyes and smiling at me before wrapping her arms around me and pulling me in for a hug.

"Hey, I lived with you long enough to know your appetite."

Addie reached out and smacked Austin across the arm, laughing. "My appetite, man, you are delusional."

"Come and get it," I yelled after I had set the pizza, wings, and paper plates onto the kitchen table.

Austin grabbed me and pulled me in front of him, my body snuggling up against him as he wrapped his arms around me while everyone came in to fill their plates with food.

"I can't wait until they are gone," he whispered into my ear, his lips grazing my earlobe, sending a chill through my body.

I elbowed him gently in the ribs and laughed.

"I want to christen every single room in this house with you," he whispered again, this time kissing my neck.

"Oh my God! Would you two get a room!" Addie said, rolling her eyes as she looked over at us. "You'll have plenty of time to do whatever it is you're whispering to Kristy about enough to make her blush."

Everyone broke out into laughter.

Hours later, the house was finally quiet, everyone having left Austin and I alone for the first time the entire day. We sat together on the couch, his arms wrapped around me, and I closed my eyes, resting my head on his chest.

I felt Austin place a gentle kiss on my shoulder. "What are you thinking about?"

"Hmmm, just how lucky I am to finally have found you," I whispered.

"Me too," he said, pulling my T-shirt down a little more off my shoulder and kissing me again.

"It's awful, but you've been in front of my face all these years. I somehow feel like I wasted them."

Austin was quiet for a minute. Then he placed his fingers under my chin, lifting my head so I could meet his eyes. "Sometimes, the things you want the most are right in front of your face all along. It just takes some time for them to appear." Slowly, he brought his lips to mine and kissed me slow and deep. When we parted he looked at me. "I'm so happy that I finally had the courage to open my eyes again enough to see you."

I stood up from the couch and held my hand out to him. He looked up at me. "What are you doing?"

I pulled my T-shirt off and unclasped my bra, allowing it to fall away from my body. "To christen the bedroom." I smiled, my cheeks heating at the thought.

Austin stood, placing his hands under my ass as he

lifted me. I wrapped my legs around his waist and kissed him. He carried me down the hall, falling into the walls as he concentrated on kissing me. Finally, we had made it to the bedroom, where he put me down onto the floor and pushed me back onto the bed. He kissed his way down to one breast, sucking and nipping my nipple with his teeth, before moving to the other. He kissed his way down my stomach, flicking the button of my jeans open and kissing his way lower. I raised my butt off the bed and he pulled my jeans off my body. I met his eyes as he opened my legs, kissing from my knee up to my inner thigh on both sides and then stood looking down on me. I could see the outline of his cock through his boxers, hard and ready to go. I could almost already feel him entering me. I wanted to feel every inch of him.

"Where are you going?" I asked, frustration reeling through me as he backed away.

"To shut the door."

"Why?"

"Because I don't want the neighbors to hear your screams, because what I want to do to you, well..."

I could feel my cheeks heat and knew I was in trouble as the door slammed shut, but trouble of the good kind. I was so excited to be on this journey with this incredible man and couldn't wait to see what our future held.

A NOTE FROM THE AUTHOR

Dear Readers,

I would like to thank you for taking the time to read *Fireside Love*. I hope you enjoyed Austin and Kristy's story. If you did, I would love it if you would drop me a review. Reviews are so important and really help me; plus I love to hear what my readers think.

Coming Soon

Holiday Wishes

ABOUT THE AUTHOR

S.L. Sterling had been an avid reader since she was a child, often found getting lost in books. Today, if she isn't writing or plotting, she can be found buried in a romance novel. S.L. Sterling lives with her husband and dogs in Northern Ontario.

Sign up for my Newsletter and get Our Little Secret FREE!

Visit my Website

Join my Street Team
Sterlings Silver Sapphires

ALSO BY S.L. STERLING

It Was Always You

On A Silent Night

Bad Company

Back to You this Christmas

The Malone Brother Series

A Kiss Beneath the Stars

In Your Arms

His to Hold

Finding Forever with You

Vegas MMA

Dagger